Sanitarium Magazine
Issue no. 21

First Published 2014 by Sanitarium Press

This edition published 2020 by Sanitarium Publishing

ISBN: 9798699881376

© 2020 Sanitarium Publishing

The right of Sanitarium Publishing to be identified as the publisher of this work has been asserted by them in accordance with the Copyright, Designs and Patents Act 1988

You may not copy, store, distribute, transmit, reproduce or otherwise make available this publication (or any part of it) in any form, or by any means (electronic, digital, optical, mechanical, photocopying, recording or otherwise), without the prior written permission of the publisher. Any person who performs any unauthorised act in relation to the contents this publication may be liable to criminal prosecution and civil claims for damages.

Facebook: https://www.facebook.com/SanitariumPublishing

2014 Edition edited by Barry Skelhorn

2020 Edition by Ian Sputnik

Thank you to all of our contributors, we couldn't have done it without you.

Contents

ISSUE TWENTY-ONE

Dear Reader,

This month's issue not only showcases up and coming writers of dark verse and fiction, it also covers this hears HWA "Bram Stoker" Awards for 2013. There is of course the old guard, but it is the new blood that is coming through that really excites me.

I can't help to think that maybe, just maybe one of the writers who have or will appear in our pages – might go on to pick up an award. One can dream right?

So thank you for picking up this month issue, we hope you enjoy the eclectic mix and please if you like what you see leave a rate or review.

Thank you again for your time and welcome to the Sanitarium.

Barry Skelhorn

Catherine

Logan Edwards

Physician: Dr. Roundtree
8245-AVD12

I CAN NEVER FORGET THOSE GREEN EYES. The shade was peculiar, nearly that of the oak leaves on a summer afternoon. I have many fond memories of them, the way those eyes would fall upon me with such delight and the care they held for me. Even as Catherine waned, her lovely eyes never lost their intensity of hue. You'll want to know the details, considering my impending trial.

The illness first manifested itself in the weeks after our wedding. She complained of mild headaches; I dismissed it as the afterglow jitters of our whirlwind courtship. I did my best to alleviate her suffering, but thought it nothing serious. But as months passed and summer came, the headaches intensified, and fatigue and loss of coordination manifested themselves. I became greatly alarmed and made an appointment with a physician at once. The doctor ordered several rounds of testing—including MRIs—but all came back negative.

A mental decline of my own paralleled Catherine's physical decline. It is of a certain familial character that I suffer visual and auditory illusions in times of stress. Whilst I am happy, they do not appear often, but are never pleasant. In the year I had known Catherine, the fiends had not appeared but once. On our wedding day, as I awaited the bride I loved dearly, the figure of Death seemed to sit in the back row of her relatives' pews.

Oh, how ghastly was His form! The sable cloak he wore seemed not even to register the light streaming through the stained-glass panes. The skin upon his hands and bald cranium stretched tightly over the bones like the desiccated skin of some preserved corpse. Those black eyes pierced through me into my soul, yet the feeling he gave through that stare was pity for me. I closed my eyes, trying to shake the illusion. The bridal march began playing. I opened my eyes and the figure had vanished, leaving me to behold my love. That wasn't the last of him, however.

However, as Catherine grew more ill, I saw death and his hobgoblins on an increasingly regular basis. Deep in the night, as my wife slept, hoping to recover, I sat in bed listening in terror to the footsteps, and giggles, and laughs, and screams that emanated throughout our estate. Nothing in the house gave token to the source of the ghoulish noises. I searched and sought feverishly while the sun was high, and even harder as it left for the night.

Catherine would often awake to encounter me silently treading the house with my unintelligible purpose. She would always grab me by the hand when she found me in that excited delirium. The noises would silence uncannily and quickly and each hallucination shatter in such a violent, sudden fashion that it was more startling than the apparitions themselves. Instantly, I would collapse into Catherine's arms and weep. Alas, why wouldn't my hellish tormentors leave me be?

Catherine's body continued to fall apart despite the best efforts of clergymen, physicians, and myself. Her strength slowly sapped by some unseen spectre, I descended deeper into the maelstrom of my own mind. I became convinced that the damned souls that pursued my waking nightmares were out to kill me through the murder of the one I lived for. Many nights, I screamed to them to take me, to destroy me, to end me, to leave my fair lady alone and harm one who could take it. It was to no effect. Catherine wasted away in my arms as I sat helpless to save her, a knight in aluminum armor.

No diagnosis came forward. Scientists spoke of rare genetic disorders, necromancers and conjurers of malevolent, vindictive spirits. Catherine remained bedridden as her strange illness progressed, and I became her nurse. I thank the Lord she began having episodes where she would blank out somewhere between sleep and consciousness, relieving her of the pain that I could see in those beautiful green eyes.

My work—research chemistry—fell to the wayside as I devoted more time to her care. Thoughts of my job came to me in the many nights of tears and turmoil I weathered. I was working with a team of other, greater scientists to develop a more effective antidote for overdoses of alkaline earth metals. The primary symptoms of magnesium poisoning are loss of consciousness followed by respiratory arrest; in other words, a quick, peaceful death. I had the syringes and the hypodermic needles. I could beckon for the magnesium solutions at any time. Most expected her passing and thus she likely would be interred without autopsy or toxicology report.

Oh Death! How you play your hand in such a way that the merciful murdering of my wife, my one and only true love, be the only escape from your domain for both spouses!

Many nights, I sat by her side and pondered the thin needle I held. It would be merely a pinprick and her suffering would be over. On more than one occasion, I brought it close to the sickly vein on the inside of her elbow, tears streaming down my face. I would aim and steady it for use, then pull back. The tiny, ethereal bit of hope for her recovery I still clung to would break my will. I'd fall asleep stroking that blonde hair, attenuated and dead as a chemo patient's.

Catherine retained her mental fortitude even as her body withered and her skin grew like that of the uninvited wedding guest. Never once did I see her cry, even when I shook and cried with her head cradled in my chest. It is ironic, isn't it, how our wedding bed, the scene of the culmination of the happiest day of our lives, would become her deathbed, the scene of the greatest tragedy. Yet she lay resolute, ready to face whatever the cold hand of fate placed upon her. I refused to accept it, however, and turned to more and more arcane resources to stave off the reaper's scythe. All failed.

I remember the day exactly, as it's burnt into my memory beyond healing. It was August 13th. The ticking cat clock read 9:14. That clock was always one of Catherine's conversation pieces, but I couldn't stand that damn thing. The morning sun gave a golden glow to the walls. I took a tray to our master bedroom to give to Catherine. I had made her breakfast on our finest china, which was a wedding gift from my estranged cousin. My cousin, Holly, was quite the belligerent sort and had repeatedly forced me to pick her up from the police department for bar brawls and such. Catherine took a shine to it and had eaten off it at least once a week since our marriage, but her favorite piece of the entire set was the little, white teacup with red and teal wildflowers on the sides. Each day, I served her orange spice tea with honey in that cup, especially as she fell ill. I placed the tray upon her lap. I had made two pancakes, eggs, and a molehill of bacon that day. After expressing our love for each other, I left to clean the kitchen. As I rinsed out the skillet, I heard a crash from our room. I sprinted with frenetic speed and nearly took our door off its hinges to find her in her final spasmodic death throes. As I approached, her breathing halted. I started CPR. I was screaming between breathes

"Breathe, damn you! Breathe!" I could hear her ribs cracking under the force of my compressions. She became a blur behind my tears as I realized the futility of my actions. All my efforts had proven fruitless. I grabbed the phone with and dialled 911, hoping to redeem her from Death. The soft, effeminate voice on the other end of the line asked me for my emergency. As though the shock had turned me into an automaton, I stated the details of her malady and fall. I felt warmth spreading across my face. I sat the phone down on the nightstand beside me.

"Sir? Are you still there?" and looked at my hands. My own blood coated them; chunks of our china imbedded at random points. In my haste, I must have grabbed the pieces and not noticed. I turned and witnessed the figure of our wedding doting over Catherine's face. Blood trails left her nose and the corners of her mouth. He looked at me and then her. I reached out to strike the dark cloaked man, but my fist passed through him. I don't remember what happened next.

The paramedics told me I was in the bed with her, holding onto her for dear life. All I remember is coming to in a hospital waiting room, my green shirt in tatters from tearing at it. The man across from me must have been a familiar of Death's as he was nothing but skin and bone. I contemplated the putrid yellow color of what flesh he had left and the tan of his bones. Was that the fate of my fair Catherine? The doctor came out and confirmed my suspicion. The radiant heroine lay slain by the mystery ailment. The words ran off my mind like water.

I declined an autopsy, fearing that it would prove as pointless an endeavor as the witches' and doctors' previous attempt to demystify the insoluble disease. The funeral came a week later. Oh, how little I remember of the funeral and its processions, yet two events are tattooed into my mind.

The viewing was one of such scenes. The ebony coffin sat parallel to the pews. Its carbon black exterior contrasted to the white fabric interior. The interior's deceptively soft look brought more comfort to mourners than to the corpse it held. The three golden rectangular outlines on either long side gave it an almost royal look, had it not been for the context of their application. On either side were bouquets of red, yellow, and white roses. She hated roses, too cliché. Had I not been too distraught to help plan the arrangements,

I would have used lavender. She always loved the smell of it. The stained-glass window gave little light upon the scene due to the stormy conditions. I felt floating, as if the carpet was not beneath me. Catherine herself lay in that box in such a peaceful fashion. I laughed despite myself and it turned into cries of anguish. She died in paroxysms and blood and they posed her as if she died from my poisoning. The dress she was wearing hung off her. My god, she had lost so much weight. I know not how long I stood by her, hours? Eventually, some minister grabbed me and shocked me out of my silent reveries and back into reality. I was the last one left in that house of worship.

The other would be the burial at Silveridge Cemetery. Quite fitting of the sepulchral rite, it rained that cursed day. I was at the side of that six-foot-deep hole. The casket had begun its final descent. Mirror-like drops of water specked the shiny, black lid of the coffin. I stared into that the abyss that separated me from my beloved. The minister began to speak, but I might as well have been deaf for sight of his companion. Catherine stood next to him plain as day. Hehe! Had I finally snapped? I turned and faced the rows of mourners behind me to see teary faces not registering my wonderfully taunting illusion. Were they blind to the sight before them? I turned back and stared into her eyes. She placed her index finger over her lips. I complied, admiring her body back in all its former glory. Her hair floated like seaweed. It was thick and full, as if she had never fallen ill. She beckoned me; her hand had cast off the pallor of the grave. I stood. With my eyes only on her, I stepped forward and landed on top of the casket. Family members were horrified and even the little frumpy pastor was caught off guard by my sudden change in altitude. Had they not known how distraught I was, they likely would've hated me for ruining the burial. I wanted to stay down it that hole, to reunite with Catherine. They pulled me out though.

After her interment, I became lucid and the fugue states that had shielded me from the full impact of grief faded. Since her death, not once had I touched the master bedroom. The last vestige of her was scattered across the floor of that room and I feared it as much as I meant to preserve it. I slept on the couch until nearly a week after the burial just because of that one wish. My phantasms failed to abate, but their nature took a radical shift.

The reaper had taken a leave of absence, but left a crueler apparition in his stead. While I didn't see her, I could feel Catherine like a perfume thickening the air. I half expected her to be there whenever I turned around or turned a corner. I reiterate that she was never there though, as if she had just moved out of my field of vision. I finally brought myself to enter our bedroom, in hopes of dissipating my spectral bride. As I entered the room, several things stood out to me.

The olive drab and dandelion comforter was disturbed and spattered with rust brown patches from my love and me. There were shards of china spread throughout the room. The only thing not in disarray was that little teacup, which had miraculously survived the destruction. It's juxtaposition against the general disorder of the room made a port in my stormy seas. I made the bed, shaking the broken pieces onto the floor, and gingerly placed the teacup on the pillow beside my own. I vacuumed up the small ceramic bits and manually removed the larger ones. I wish I could've kept them in that room, but couldn't as they would merely serve as cutting reminders of the incident. I crawled into bed for the night, that little teacup beside me.

That night was a new moon. I woke up some time after midnight to a great crash that jolted me from my fitful sleep. I opened the nightstand drawer as silently as possible and withdrew the revolver. I grabbed the munitions, .38 special, from the box that lay near it in that drawer. I loaded each round and locked the cylinder into place. I got out of bed, trying to avoid the noise of the box springs, and tiptoed to the door. I cocked the gun and opened the door. The noise seemed to come from the kitchen and I duck walked in that direction. I checked and found empty every doorway on my way, but the stillness and silence painted a streak of hostility on the environment. I stepped into the kitchen, gun drawn, and flicked the light switch. I was the only one in the room. The clock was shattered on the floor. I squatted down and examined the remains. Someone must have thrown or smashed the clock, as the damage was much too extensive to result from a fall. I straightened up and searched the rest of the house for the clock's assailant. However, I had locked every door and window and not a trace of a living being other than me presented itself. Quite shaken, I returned to our room and locked the door.

Night regained its ability to inflict terror upon me and I heard noises throughout the house, even during the daylight hours. The noises were much more familiar than the previous set. They sounded more like someone living in the house than the twisted nature of Death's brood. Once one morning, I awoke to hear my kitchen faucet running. I jumped out of bed and ran to the kitchen to shut it off. The basin and drain were dry and the knobs were off when I reached it. The teacup was sitting on the drain, and seeing it there when I know I had placed it in the cupboard yesterday made my blood like ice in my veins. I grabbed it and left to return it to its place. The noises intensified as I have just described on rare occasions, but that damned teacup always found its way to the scene. One night, after another sink incident, I steeled my nerves and rushed in to take the cup. Catherine was in the kitchen this time. I froze and barely avoided swooning. She gave me a smile before turning around, entering the next room through a thick honey locust door, and closing it with a creak. I professed my love to her and threw the door open, only to reveal that teacup. What was so special about it? How was it getting around the house? Had I had any time unaccounted for? How would I even know if I did lose consciousness? Was she a figment of a cracked mind? Was my lady resurrected to console me? Why? Why must she be so mysterious? Couldn't she just tell me? I would've smashed that cup had it not been for my sentimentality.

I took an unhealthy interest in the cup, so that even the noises and apparitions of Catherine did not get more than a glance from me. I took that little cup to a nearby university for identification and found out it was an 18th century Italian piece. I had taken some ceramics in high school and picked clay up once again as I learned the precise specifications and techniques used to make that cup. In my broken mind, maybe I could appease Catherine if I made her more cups. My mental faculty was almost broken away from reality at this point and my reasoning carried the same train of thought as the Winchester mansion. I ordered 200 pounds of clay, a kiln, and the needed glazes and began working at a psychotic tempo in my basement. Even as I built more and more, the hallucination of Catherine refused to relent and her spirit remained stuck on that one cup. The revelation came one day while I was glazing cup #234.

I noted the white glaze was marked for use on decorative surfaces only. Oh, how my obsession had narrowed my vision. I took the teacup, chipped a small piece from the bottom, and took it to work. I dissolved the chip in hydrofluoric, then nitric acid. I added potassium iodide and a yellow precipitate formed, the cup's glaze contained lead.

It all made sense now; she had heavy metal poisoning. My cousin's gift had poisoned her. I loaded the revolver; I went to several different stores buying lighters, duct tape, and a razor blade. I threw my tools into the lap of Death, who was sitting in my passenger seat (he was an old friend to me by this point), and… Well, you know the rest, don't you detective? You've read the police report. How I threw my cousin down her basement stairs and torture-murdered her the way she did Catherine? How I ignored her pleas of mercy? How it took two weeks for her to die? Why yes I'm guilty, but I'll plead innocent. You think I can get off on an insanity defense? No, I'll pass your shrink. Just tell the D.A. to seek the death penalty; I just want Catherine.

The End.

Case #19951
Logan Edwards

Logan Edwards is an undergraduate chemistry student in Indiana with a minor in creative writing. He enjoys exercise and watching scary movies.

CLAYTON HILL SANITARIUM

Carbon Copy

Peter Emmett Naughton

Physician: Dr. Peterson
8268-WCT29

Lisa looked down at the tips of her fingers and made another attempt to clean them, but the ink just smudged around on her skin leaving her hands stained and stinking of toner. 'What was the point of having high-tech laser printers if the damn things shit the bed every time a piece of paper got jammed?'

Even worse than the constant jamming was the complete mess they made of things when you tried to clear them out. She might as well be back in the manual type setting days using lead stencils and a hand-crank printing press; at least then she'd have a reasonable excuse for looking and smelling like an ink-stained wretch.

"That's just fucking perfect." Lisa muttered to herself as she stared at the muddy gray swirls on her palms.

She was supposed to meet her roommate for drinks after work, but she sure as hell didn't want to show up looking like a victim of the black plague or like she'd gnawed off the top of her pen.

"Vinegar."

Lisa jumped at the voice and turned around to see one of the custodians, a white-haired woman who couldn't have been much more than four feet tall, emptying the large garbage can in the office break room.

"I'm sorry, what was that you said?"

"I've got a bottle of vinegar in the utility closet; it should do the trick. I'll go ahead and grab it for you."

"Oh, thank you, that'd be great."

"Be back in a sec." the custodian said and she turned and pushed her cart out of the room and around the corner.

Lisa went over to the faucet in the break room and started working on her fingertips again. She could picture herself cleaning ink off her hands for the next thirty years and the thought made her shudder. It wasn't that her job was bad, in fact it had been the best gig she'd ever had, but it wasn't what she wanted to do with her life.

'Well what exactly do you want to do with your life?'

Her mother would invariably ask this question every time she and Lisa went out to dinner and Lisa never had an answer that satisfied her. This frustrated her mother to no end and Lisa had to bite her tongue to stop herself from reminding her mother that her own life plan thus far had consisted of marrying well and divorcing even better. She was sure that her mother wanted her to follow in her footsteps, though obviously not the latter part despite how nicely it had worked out for her financially.

There wasn't much Lisa could remember about her father. Her parent's had divorced when she was six and even before then her dad hadn't been around much, but what little she did recall of him was all good. Trips to the roller rink, the beach, the zoo, and always the ice cream shop afterward.

Her mother had insisted that it was her father's way of buying her off for being absent all the time, but that never mattered much to Lisa.

"Here you go." the custodian said, handing Lisa a large plastic bottle. "Just return it to the utility closet when you're done."

"Thanks again, you're a real-life saver." "My pleasure dearie."

Lisa watched as the woman rounded the corner and disappeared down the corridor. She turned back to the sink and splashed some of the vinegar on her hands, sighing in relief as the ink started to come off.

Her phone buzzed and she quickly wiped the water and vinegar off her fingers and dug her cell out of her purse.

"Hello?"

"Hey stranger, where ya been?"

"Hey Amy, I'm still at work. I'm sorry, I meant to call, but things just got crazy around here."

"Yeah, yeah, what else is new; so, are you still coming?"

"After the day I've had, I don't think I'd be able to make it without some form of alcoholic assistance."

"That's what I like to hear."

"I should be outta here in a few minutes."

"I'll have a beer waiting for you when you get here."

"And that is why you are the best roommate in the whole wide world."

"Damn, I was bucking for galaxy, maybe even universe." "We'll talk about a promotion after my second beer."

***

By the time Lisa was on her third beer she had managed to stop staring at the faint stain that remained on her fingers, though the sharp smell of vinegar was hard for her to ignore.

"Alright Lis, out with it." Amy said.

"Out with what?"

"Don't pretend like you don't know what I'm talking about. You've been totally zoned since you got here."

"I just had a crappy day."

"Every day at that place has been crappy. So why are you still letting it make you miserable?"

"The job market is a total mess right now."

"If you keep waiting for the perfect time to jump ship, you're gonna wind up with a shitty little retirement package and an apartment full of cats."

"Hey, we've only got two cats."

"Yeah, because I stopped you at two. Also, totally missing my point."

"I know, it's just...."

"Look, I get that you haven't figured out exactly what you want right now, but you know that the place you're at isn't it, and it's not like the pay is all that great, right?"

"I definitely don't want to talk about

that." So what's keeping you there?"

"Cowardice?"

"Dude, you took me to every noisy punk show, seedy dive bar, and cockroach-infested diner I've ever been to. I would've been a dorm hermit all through college if it wasn't for you dragging me to awesome stuff that scared the living shit out of me."

"This is different."

"I know it is, and I know you're worried, but I hate seeing you like this."

"I just need to get a few things in order and then I'm gonna start looking again."

"Promise?"

"Cross my heart."

"Hope to die, stick a needle in your eye?"

"Let's leave out the death wish and the inter-ocular trauma; I'd rather not risk jinxing myself right now."

"Alright, I'll let you off easy this time. Another round?"

"I should really head home. I have to be in early tomorrow to finish up some things."

"Big blinking neon sign Lis; Get. Out. Now."

"I'll see ya back at our place. Call me if you need a ride later." "Doesn't that sort of defeat the purpose of you leaving early?" "Well then at least call a cab if you need to, okay?" "Yeah, yeah, alright mom."

"Pretty sure your mother never took you to see Bratmobile at the Empty Bottle."

"No, but she did take me to see New Kids on the Block when I was eight."

"That explains so much."

"Yeah, like I don't know about that Tiffany poster you still have tucked away in your closet."

"Hey, Tiffany was reflecting the banality of consumerism by holding concerts in shopping malls. She was practically a proto riot girl, not like that preppie Debbie Gibson."

"I believe she goes by Deborah now." "Whatever, Electric Youth still sucked."

"Agreed. Now get outta here before we start talking about Menudo."

"What, no New Edition?"

"I'm putting the pin back in this nostalgia grenade before it explodes. Back away slowly and I'll see you at home."

"Okay, okay, I'm going. Text me when you're leaving."

"I will. Later on Tiff."

"See ya Deb."

Lisa blew Amy a kiss and then quickly exited the bar before Amy had a chance to respond with a comeback. On the drive back to her apartment she had a burning urge to listen to I Think We're Alone Now, but the thought of actually purchasing the track made her feel silly and self conscious.

At home she scrubbed at her hands with liquid soap until the scent of lavender overpowered the sharp tang of the vinegar. The toner was gone now except for the faintest traces that still clung underneath her nails and in between the grooves of her fingers, but she knew that it was only a temporary reprieve.

'Well at least now I know how to get rid of the stuff.'

The thought wasn't very comforting. It made her wonder how many more times her hands would need to undergo the vinegar treatment and her mind flashed again to the image of herself thirty years on standing over the sink in the office break room.

She knew Amy was right. There was no reason for her to still be at her job. It was the first real offer she'd gotten out of college and she took it because she was tired of working retail and afraid something better might not come along. Since then she'd put out a handful of resumes here and there and gone on a few interviews, but the truth is that she hadn't been looking all that hard. She'd set up a profile on one of those job search engines, but by the time she got home her brain felt fried and she barely had the mental wherewithal left to go online and comb through the pile of potential matches, much less actually pursue any of them.

Her laptop had actually become something of a source of dread for her. She had begun actively avoiding it after work so she wouldn't feel guilty about not checking her profile page.

Lisa opened the door to her bedroom, glancing over at the computer sitting on her desk, before changing into her pajamas and climbing into bed. She grabbed the book on top of her nightstand and riffled through the pages until she found the torn iced tea label she'd been using as a bookmark.

On page twenty-three a low-level thug enforcer was beating the hell out of a junkie who was behind on his bill. It was early in the story and Lisa wasn't sure if either of these two would turn out to be the protagonist or even a major character, but so far she was rooting for the drug fiend with the bloody nose.

***

Lisa arrived at work before the sun was up and had almost finished everything from the night before by the time the first of the nine-to-five regulars had come in.

The last thing she needed to do was print copies of her report for the meeting that morning. She crossed her fingers, checked the collate box, and clicked print.

Three pages in the printer made a loud clicking sound followed by a low whir and then an orange light on the front of the machine started blinking.

"Oh come on!" Lisa said, louder than she'd intended.

The woman who sat next to Lisa peered over the top of her cube, but quickly ducked back down when she saw the expression on Lisa's face.

'Maybe it's just out of paper or the toner is running low?'

But she was all too familiar with the sound the machine had made, and she knew that it wasn't either of those things.

She marched over and stared incredulously at the tiny black and white display.

JAM IN REGION 2. PLEASE OPEN TOP OF MACHINE AND REMOVE OBSTRUCTION.

"I hate you, you fucking piece of shit." Lisa said through gritted teeth.

She rolled up the sleeves of her blouse and flipped open the top panel of the machine. Inside was a long, thin piece of molded gray plastic, which she pulled out to reveal the angular black ink cartridge underneath. Removing it required her to release two small latches on either side of it and the moment she touched the first one she could feel the powdery toner smear onto her fingertips.

She bit back the urge to scream and removed the toner cartridge, placing it on the table next to her. In the space where the toner had been there was a shiny metal flap that ran the length of the printer and underneath it was the mangled remains of page four from her report. It took several minutes to fish out all the scraps of paper and by the time she had reassembled the printer she barely had enough time to wipe off her hands and reprint everything for the meeting.

The rest of the day passed in a blur. She managed to get through her portion of the presentation, but had a difficult time paying attention for the remainder of the meeting and what she did hear sounded like bees droning inside her head. On the way home she stopped at the store to pick up a bottle of vinegar and a small, wooden-handled brush that was meant for cleaning cuticles.

She stared into her kitchen sink and slowly poured the vinegar over her fingers, scrubbing at them with the tiny brush. The vinegar at work had been clear, but this was brown and had a faintly sweet smell to it, though it was no less pungent.

It took longer this time to remove the stains from her hands, but eventually the ink began to fade and by the time she cracked open her first beer it had mostly vanished from her skin.

"Lisa, you home? Lis?"

Amy had a load of groceries in her arms that she just managed to get to the kitchen counter before dropping them.

"Hey, space cadet." Amy said.

"Huh?"

"Did you not hear me calling you the first six times?" "Oh, uh, sorry I was just...."

"Don't sweat it. So how was work?" "It was okay."

"Actually okay, or barely-tolerable okay?" "I don't really remember."

"How many beers have you had?" "Just a couple."

"I was thinking spaghetti for dinner. If you wanna boil some water, I'll get started on the sauce."

Lisa downed the last of her beer and made her way over to the sink. She reached up to grab a pot from the rack above the counter and that's when she noticed it; a black streak about six inches long running along the front hallway.

"What are you staring at?" Amy said.

Lisa pointed at the ink smudge.

"Did you do that?"

"I don't know. I didn't think I touched the wall when I came home, but...."

"Oh well, no biggie."

"I'm really sorry."

"Seriously, it's not worth worrying about. Worst comes to worst we can just paint over it."

"I just don't understand how it got there."

"You probably didn't even realize you were doing it." "Yeah, I guess."

***

Lisa didn't even look over at her computer as she got ready for bed. She glanced at the book on her nightstand, but she didn't feel much like picking it up either. She was exhausted and only

24

wanted sleep, had felt that way for most of the day, but still didn't think she was tired enough to have smeared ink all over the wall without knowing it. On the way home from work she'd made sure not to touch her steering wheel with her fingertips to avoid staining it, so why would she suddenly forget the second she walked in the door?

That night she dreamt that she was standing in front of her kitchen sink trying to scrub the black stains from her hands again, only this time the ink wouldn't come off. Instead it began to spread down her palms, oozing past her wrists and around her elbows, slithering up towards her shoulders like a pair of black snakes racing to sink their fangs into the sides of her neck.

She woke covered in a sheen of sweat and spent the rest of the night tossing and turning.

***

When her alarm went off at six the next morning Lisa had already been fully awake for almost an hour. The early gray light slanting in through her window illuminated the dust motes floating in the air and she stared at them fixated until the buzzing of her bedside clock finally shook her from her trance.

Her throat felt dry and scratchy and she wondered if she was getting a cold; it certainly wouldn't surprise her if her immune system was as worn out as the rest of her. She stumbled to the bathroom with her eyes still half closed and cupped her palms under the tap. Lisa suddenly had a mental flash of black ink pouring from the faucet instead of water and had to fight the urge not to spit it back into the sink.

A part of her wanted to forget about work and call in sick, but that would just leave her frantic the next day trying to play catch-up. She was also afraid of how it would look to her boss.

'There you go again, worrying over a job that you don't even want.' she thought as she hunted around the apartment for her keys.

The office was usually locked when she got there, except on the days when the cleaning service came in, but today the building was dark when she pulled into the parking lot. The sun had finally managed to make its way over the horizon and Lisa looked at the pink and orange clouds and wanted to sink into them. Her eyelids drooped and fluttered and her legs felt like they were encased in concrete whenever she tried to move them.

Being the first one in meant she was obligated by office law to start the first pot of coffee. It also meant she could make it as strong as she liked without having to deal with the gripes and whines from those folks who wanted a pot of decaf or half-caff. It made no sense to her why anyone would voluntarily drink coffee without caffeine, but then again, some peculiar souls also drank alcohol-free beer.

"The world is a very strange place filled with very strange people." Lisa said to herself and thought about the dark stain streaked across the wall in her apartment.

It still disturbed her that she had no memory of leaving the mark; there wasn't even a vague feeling of déjà vu when she pictured herself running her inky fingertips along the smooth white surface of the front hallway.

When she was a kid she had once had a conversation with her mother late at night that she couldn't remember the next morning. Her Mom said that Lisa had been talking about giants in the clouds from a story they had read in school, but Lisa didn't recall a word of it. Still, there had been a fuzzy spot in her head that seemed to understand that it was true. She couldn't pick out any of the details, but the idea that it had happened made sense to her.

With the ink there was nothing. It was as if she had been knocked unconscious walking through the front door and then come to in front of the kitchen sink. The middle part, the part where she would have smeared toner on the wall, was completely gone, spliced clean from her memory like a piece of celluloid left on the cutting room floor.

'I really think you ought to see someone.' That's what her mother would say. 'Make an appointment with your G.P., or better yet, consult a specialist.' Her mother undoubtedly knew the names of at least two top neurologists in the area.

But it wasn't as if she had passed out. She hadn't hit her head and woken up on the floor. She had no cuts, bumps, or bruises and she wasn't suffering from headaches or seeing spots or bright flashes.

She just couldn't remember.

The incident kept creeping into her subconscious. She would find herself reconstructing the possible permutations of the scene over and over again in her head as she stared at spreadsheets or scrutinized an email she was about to send.

'Did she use her left hand or her right?'

Coming in the hallway would have been on her left, but she was right-handed and could have reached over.

'How many fingers had she used to make the mark and which ones?'

The more she thought about it, the more she could see herself running her fingertips along the corridor. It was the same way she felt anytime something odd happened. She immediately tried to recall if the same thing had happened before, as if the simple act of repetition somehow rendered it normal and safe.

By the end of the day she had convinced herself that she had done it, despite still having no memory of the event. In the absence of any other plausible explanation it was the only thing that made any sense.

On her way home she stopped off at the grocery store for some cold medicine, a box of chamomile tea bags, and one of those magic eraser sponges she'd seen on TV that purported to get any stain out of any surface. When she walked through her front door she nearly dropped the plastic bag she was holding.

The ink had changed.

The smudge was bigger than it had been, much bigger. What had once been a short, thin streak was now a black swath at least four inches high and almost two feet across. The edges of the thing shimmered in the overhead hall light and looked viscous and fluid, more like oil or tar than ink.

'When had this happened?'

Clearly it had been after she and Amy had left for work, since there was no way that either of them could have missed something this obvious. She reached out to touch the streak half expecting her hand to come back damp and stained, but the surface was dry. When she looked down at her fingertips there was no new residue on them, though she swore she had felt a tingling, like a mild electrical current running up her arm.

"Hey Lis, you okay? You left the front door open."

Lisa turned to Amy who was locking the deadbolt behind her.

"Tell me you see this?"

"See what?"

Lisa pointed to the mark on the wall.

"Jeez, did you nail the same spot on your way in again? You've gotta start wearing gloves at work or something."

"So you see it, that it's bigger?"

"Kinda hard to miss."

"It wasn't me. I swear the wall was like this when I got here." "I don't think we're gonna get our security deposit back." "This isn't funny."

"Just calm down and relax for a second. We can go and get a can of that paint for covering up stains. I'm sure the landlord won't even notice."

"But why is it bigger?" Lisa said, trying to keep the note of hysteria out of her voice.

"It probably just leeched into the drywall and spread out."

"This morning it was the same size it had been last night, I'm sure of it."

"It probably just took a while to seep in." "But...."

"Listen Lis, you need to step back from this and take a breath. All the stress from your job is making you crazy and you're letting it freak you out over nothing. I'll take care of the wall tomorrow. Why don't you go and try and get some rest?"

"...yeah...alright...."

"Things will be better tomorrow, I promise."

***

Lisa avoided looking at the ink stain on her way out the door the next morning and made a conscious effort not to think about it on her drive in to work.

Whenever she found herself thinking about the smear on the wall, she would nibble at the inside of her mouth to distract herself; by lunchtime the interior of her lower lip was dotted from end to end with tiny blood blisters the color of ripe plumbs.

She couldn't go home; couldn't face the thought that the stain might have grown even larger.

'Maybe it had taken over the entire hallway by now, or even spread to the kitchen?'

After work Lisa went to the bar that she and Amy frequented. Instead of looking over the beer list to see what was on tap that night, she ordered a bourbon. She drained the tumbler in front of her in two long swallows, barely tasting the burning, amber liquid, and then ordered another.

The bartender cut her off after her fourth drink and called a cab for her. On the ride home she thought of asking the driver to drop her off at a motel or a friend's house, but she couldn't focus long enough to come up with a name or address.

After several moments of fumbling with her keys, she finally managed to get the door open and was hit in the face by a reeking chemical stench. She felt the liquor take a tumble in her stomach, and for a moment thought she might lose it, but quickly managed to get the urge under control.

"There you are?!" Amy said. "Christ, I was about to start phoning hospitals!"

"Sorry, the time sorta got away from me." Lisa said, slurring her words slightly. "What are you doing?"

"I told you I'd take care of it." Amy said and made a sweeping gesture at the wall.

Lisa walked in front of the spot where the stain had been and saw that it was now covered by a large square of bright white paint that was still wet and shiny.

"See, good as new." Amy said. "Well, it probably won't match the exact shade when it dries, but I don't think the super will notice."

Lisa stared at the wall for several moments and then turned and hugged Amy tight enough to knock the wind out of her.

"Thank you." Lisa said.

Amy hugged her back. "It's going to be okay. Whatever it is, I'm here for you."

"I know." Lisa said and gave Amy a final squeeze before letting go. "You want some dinner, or are you too hammered to eat?" "Actually, food sounds pretty good."

"I vote we go out somewhere so we can flee from this stink." "Anywhere you want, my treat."

"Remind me to get you shitfaced more often."

***

The paint did its job. There was no sign of the black ink bleeding through the newly applied layer of white or any trace of it spreading beyond the edges of the square that now stood out like some modernist white-on-white painting in an Art gallery.

Lisa took Amy's advice and started wearing latex gloves anytime she had to dismantle the printer. It earned her a few odd stares from her co-workers in the beginning, but she didn't care and over time people stopped noticing, or at least became more discreet with their sidelong glances and whispers.

Work was still as monotonous as it had been, but solving her printer problem helped put everything else into perspective and made the whole job feel more manageable and less like a prison sentence. She spruced up her online resume and started combing through the search engine for open positions and had even sent out a few query letters. She settled into her new routine, which still usually ended with beers at the bar with Amy after work, and for a while everything seemed better.

And then it came back.

It was subtle at first; a dark shape at the periphery of her vision that she mistook for a shadow or some trick of the light. Over time the shape began to creep in more and more until eventually it was always there, flitting in and out of her sightline like a phantom fly she could never quite catch. It got so bad that she made an appointment with an ophthalmologist, convinced she had a detached retina or some kind of corneal abrasion in one or both of her eyes.

The ophthalmologist told her that there was nothing physically wrong with her vision and her general physician confirmed the diagnosis when she went for a second opinion. After the appointment her G.P. had recommended a colleague in the mental health field, but Lisa never went to see her.

Whatever this was, she knew that it wasn't just in her head.

She'd barely even thought about the ink stain since Amy had painted over it. In truth it had never really been about the stain anyway. During dinner that night with Amy she had poured everything out. The frustrations with work that she had tried to downplay, her feelings of insecurity over her future, and the fact that she was secretly afraid that her mother was right about her.

It had all manifested itself through that smear on the wall, which she was still sure she had made and simply not remembered it. She admitted to Amy that she had 'gone a little bonkers' and Amy had accepted this explanation, and why shouldn't she? After all, it was the truth.

Specialist after specialist told Lisa that there was nothing wrong with her eyes or the wiring in her brain. The shadows had begun to take on a more solid form. Now instead of darting from place to place, they oozed around the edges of her visual frame, never quite centered enough to focus on, but never entirely absent either. Even when she closed her eyes she could still sense them, pulsing under her lids like the after-image left by the sun if you stared straight up at it and didn't blink.

Her sleep was plagued by nightmares of an enveloping black liquid that surrounded and slowly drowned her. The shadow substance poured over her mouth and nose, filling her throat and lungs until there wasn't even enough air left for her to choke. In the dream she could feel the inky substance permeating her pores and pushing into the sockets of her eyes.

She always woke to her sheets drenched in sweat, usually coughing up air and spit and feeling like she was still suffocating.

Amy tried to talk to her about it, but Lisa kept quiet, insisting that everything was fine. Their relationship became more and more strained until Amy finally moved out after a huge fight that had ended with Amy begging Lisa to get some professional help.

Shortly after that Lisa stopped wearing the gloves at work. She let the toner from the cartridges stain her hands and made no attempt to wash it off; she simply didn't see the point.

She made a new smear in the place where the old one had been and followed it with several others. The apartment walls were soon covered in black streaks and smudges, though none of them ever changed shape or seemed to shimmer around the edges like the original.

The dreams changed too. In them she was still being smothered by a nebulous black mass, but the sensation of suffocation had been replaced by a pleasant, creeping warmth that felt soothing and she found herself not fighting the feeling as her consciousness slowly slipped away and she awoke feeling wooly-headed and euphoric.

At work she had become nearly comatose and had stopped answering her emails and phone calls. After a few weeks they forced her to go on paid medical leave and she never returned.

The walls in the apartment were now more black than white. She had stolen several of the toner cartridges from work and had bashed them to pieces with a hammer, smearing her hands and arms with the inky contents until she was covered up to her elbows and then spreading it onto every available surface.

The shadows had become a continuous unbroken shroud over her vision that filtered everything through its gauzy veil.

Lisa could feel the dark carbon writhing around inside her body, pulsing through her veins and pounding in her temples. It was everywhere now, a part of her.

Sitting on the edge of her bed, she looked around her room and noticed a thin rectangle of white on the opposite wall just below the window frame.

She grabbed one of the plastic toner cartridges sitting on the floor and ripped off the protective plastic lip at the front. She splayed her fingers along the length, letting the powdery, black toner work itself into the grooves and whorls of her fingers.

Lisa crept over to the sill and ran the tips of her fingers over the white strip, carefully filling it in until it was perfect.

The End.

Case #30821
Peter Emmett Naughton

Peter first fell into fiction penning stories to amuse his grammar-school classmates, which helped him overcome his shyness, but resulted in very few completed homework assignments.

He was raised and currently resides in the Chicagoland suburbs with his wife and cats. His writing has appeared in The Delinquent, Candlelight, Black Words On White Paper, Spook City, Apiary, Crack The Spine, Chicago Literati, Cemetery Moon, Pavor Nocturnus, and Graze.

CLAYTON HILL SANITARIUM

The Cheap Seats

Anastasia

Physician: Dr. Edgar
9828-SJE41

THE BLOOD AND SALT ON HER TOP LIP FUELLED her objective, coagulating to a gooey blur. Her brain echoed: Get out, get out now and don't look back. Lita glanced behind her shoulder, searching for a non-existent window. Outside, the pavement roasted beneath the raging sun. Lita licked her swollen lower lip. She didn't see the metal broom handle. It stung her face Kneeling, she crawled toward a breakfast cereal display.

Aisle 10: Toiletries, female sanitary products, vitamins and painkillers.

She thought she had to be insane. Then her son returned to her mind.

"Mommy you have to do it. The kids at school…"

Lita muttered. "I'm not as fit as I was…" If she had to be specific about things, then she had let herself go. Now as she crawled on her knees, her mind groaned in response to her strained stomach and fatigued thigh muscles. The things that parents yielded to, she thought. The survival of children, of familial DNA, dominated most decisions.

A month before, her son Jet finished another school day, to return in tears.

"The kids at school. Those

kids…" Lita shook her head.

"They're nice to me now…after…" and Jet let it all out. The kids didn't bully him after her name was drawn from the prize draw. His tears flowed from excitement.

"But I didn't enter the competition," Lita had said, tapping her forehead with her index finger in an effort to dislodge the memory. Aisle Madness dominated the reality ratings. Reality television was all they had. It existed to aid people like them, those struggling to stretch the basic necessities.

"It'll be fun, mom!" Jet's eyes beamed. "We'll be famous and when you win, we'll never want again!"

In no time Lita's neighbors congratulated her. she'd be a star they'd said. You'll never worry about food again…If you win.

The voice screened, dragging Lita into the present.

"Aw honey! Hunnnneyyy!" Macho, raw and laced with malcontent, the voice slithered through each aisle, penetrating three rows of canned mushrooms. "Lookie there. We're on TV!"

Lita craned her head. Krazy Jay Larkin materialized in holographic form. Her head ached. It was the show to end all shows. Sharp and beyond realistic, it reflected contemporary society and Jay Larkin was the man.

"Don't forget to visit our sponsors folks. Yes...We're back! The suspense will literally...Kill one of our contestants!"

The crowd roared. Lita's intestines churned the last few droplets of instant chicken from aisle 12.

Soup for the soul...

She pocketed the extra pack; she'd need it for her basket. Collect seven items, beat your contender (preferably to a bloody pulp) and win the prize to end all prizes: A lifetime supply of food.

"Li-ta! Li-ta!" A band of women cheered in synch.

Krazy Jay smiled.

Lita multi-tasked. Her ear fell to the ground and she squinted at the holograph.

"What do we have here? What's your

name?" "Jet."

"What say you, Jet? Lita or

Dylan?" "Mommy's on TV!"

"Lita Gardiner is your mother? Wow viewers, you heard it here first."

"Mommy!"

"Erm, yes..." Krazy Jay elbowed Jet out of the way.

Bastard, she thought. She snatched a box of painkillers, keeping her eyes riveted to the north wing: Fresh fruit and vegetables...Twenty dollars per pound. Five more items remained.

"Sweetie...Honey! I'm up to item number 4. Rosehip tea. The kind that rich folk prefer. Soothes their psyche. I'll pick some daffodils next. How you doin'?" Brillo's voice boomed, but Brillo wasn't his real name. Lita baptized him due to his wiry hair. It reminded her of Brillo pads she used to scrub her aluminum saucepans.

Krazy Jay couldn't help being repetitive. He was on the corporate payroll.

"To recap..."

I can do that for you, Lita thought. Krazy Jay feverishly outlined the rules for the third time.

Aisle Madness was the apt name of the game. The 22nd century innovation distracted the starving masses by pairing hapless worker drones with the deranged. Top Chef without the cook top, the game pitted two contenders in one supermarket and followed the mayhem live. Shown daily at the early evening timeslot, it rated higher than the evening news. Advertisers flocked to the show that promised the impossible to folks like Lita or SPLEPs: Single Parent Low Earning Proles.

The SPLEPs slipped through the social cracks, hocking their automobiles when no other alternative fuels remained. At least she had her feet. Losing the car wasn't all that bad. Lita shed forty pounds. All the walking did her good and even if it didn't build a professional athlete, her lungs functioned better since she could no longer afford cigarettes.

Think of all the positives...

She'd always return to her wise nugget. Jet switched off most evenings. The positives? He walked five miles to school without fail and she accompanied him during winter. Rain, hail or sleet. She eventually took up running – there were few alternatives Aisle Madness became a television staple. Lita envied each winner. They were admirable. Courageous even. One had to be if one was to survive the deranged. Civilians didn't compete with other civilians. It would be too simple. They were matched with psychopaths like Brillo.

1 x Aspirin, 2 sachets chicken soup...so far so good. The remaining items on her random list pained her:

3 x Melons

4 x Clothes pegs

5 x Doggie Din-Din cans

2 x Hershey's Cookies and Cream.

A gargantuan feat, gathering her items required a marathon journey covering twenty aisles, excluding the arty displays. Lita willed Krazy Jay away, but he materialized behind her.

"Lita! How are you?"

Reality shows adored mind games. Brillo could have disappeared. Where did he go?

"Busy Jay."

Before she could end her thought with, "Screw You," she noticed a gray shadow. It slid over the polished floor in the dairy section. Lita leaned to her left.

"Five more items left Lita. How are you

faring?" Keep trying Brill, Lita thought.

She shook her head, thought that she tasted her own bile. She focused on the shadow and quashed her tendency to respond. Brillo craved her voice to locate her body. He didn't have a shopping list. He didn't need on when she was his only item.

Lita estimated a ten foot gap between her and the dairy section. Brillo wasn't deaf. He was toying with her. His soft bulk came into view. He leaned over, picked up a quart of milk, unscrewed the top and eagerly sculled like a starving boy.

Krazy Jay's amplified voice hovered above them.

"Lita is watching her opponent. Shhh…We mustn't disturb them and ruin the suspenseful moment--"

"Shut up," she hissed.

"Tut-tut…I say, how are you finding Dylan Stephenson? Is he as tough as they say?"

Dylan Stephenson.

His name was so ordinary. As ordinary as the drones that entered data and processed work passes at The Human Services Bureau.

"You know how to pick them," she replied. Lita crawled away from the holographic pain in her ass.

"I see you Lita…Lita is heading to the confectionary

section." Tell the world. Bastard.

Krazy Jay expected Brillo-Dylan to turn, abandon his thirst and chase her through the aisles. Lita knew otherwise. Dylan Stephenson. The name not only rang bells, it shattered glass. Was a lifetime supply of food worth the ordeal? They'd return Dylan to his maximum-security hidey-hole after he achieved…

Lita shook her head. Stop it, don't doubt. You can take him. Chocolate is sweet, she thought, but nothing was sweeter than seeing the Hershey's bar two feet away and grabbing her required quantity. She'd leave the melon last. Three melons! They sure made it difficult. She'd balance all three on her head if she had to. Anything to reach the finish line.

"Missy! Oh Missy…Here, kitty."

The holographic footage of the audience and television host shifted to the periphery of her brain. "Dylan's psyching Lita out…"

"That's my Mommy!"

"Lita…Aw Lita…I wanna do stuff to ya…Maybe with this drain cleaner. I'll fix you a cocktail of equal parts cleaner and tonic water. Add a twist of lemon, a maraschino cherry. Give you a squeeze and…Hey presto…don't have a squirrel up my sleeve. We'll have a Bloody Lita!" His laughter crawled toward her like a wounded dog. She preferred to be dipped in a vat of roaches. What unnerved her more wasn't his threat but his overdone faux Southern accent.

Lita crawled behind the canned Roma tomato display. The retro pyramid would serve as a sixty second pit stop. If she correctly recalled news histories, Brillo stood at six feet and six inches. His voice emanated from the breakfast cereal aisle four aisles away. She willed her trembling lips to stop. Breathe in…through your nose… breath out through your nose. The deranged freak is breathing down your neck. Why didn't you give Jet a clip around the ear, ground him for the rest of his natural life…sell him to the labor agents. He'd work in China…

Guilt stabbed her.

I'm a terrible mother, I know but what the fuck was he thinking? Like all children, Jet weighed the pros against the cons. Lita briefly considered her pros. Tough enough to wrestle her volatile husband to the floor, she disarmed him as Jet summoned the police. She worked two jobs, both amounting to sixteen hours a day. When the economy trudged along, failing to bounce back to its dismal late 21st century form, many ended their lives. This reminder buckled others down. The world citizens resigned themselves to a lifetime of corporate serfdom.

Brillo screamed. "I'm almost there, honey!"

Peering up over the stacked cans, she held her breath and considered the benefits the cans presented. She had time to race to the nearest checkout. She had to believe that even if her limbs worked against her. She reached up and transferred as many cans into her basket.

"Here I go," she whispered, comforted by her resilient walking shoes. People abandoned prayer decades ago. Lita didn't care. She channeled positive thoughts. Even if she made it to the checkout and back to the canned tomato stack, it would be a life changing contribution. That was all that mattered.

Lita looked both ways. There were two aisles to her left and twelve to her right. She immediately knew how resources ran out. How could the world continue with so many aisles, products and product lines? Stop thinking about things you can't control!

She raced forward, gripping the metal basket handles. Her knuckles screamed. When she reached the vacant checkout, she dropped the basket and turned toward her right. Behind…behind…ooh shit! Fear gripped her body hair; her forearms prickled and her heart beat felt like one long spasm. Certain she'd see Brillo standing behind her with a garden rake or hoe aimed at her head, she whipped her head around.

Nothing.

Phew. Thank Christ, God and the Virgin Mother.

She sprinted to the next aisle, eyed the painkillers and dropped them into her basket. The thought that spliced her brain related to the other checkout counters. Brillo placed raw meat products on each counter. A lamb's brain, a rack of lamb and an entire fillet of beef. Clearly taunting her, she kept her eyes averted and considered the remaining items on her list. The clothes pegs were dead easy. The Doggie Din Dins presented the next grueling challenge. There were no baskets to aid her between the aisles. Once the baskets were deposited at the counters, that was it. If there were no baskets near the aisles, it was just too bad. Lita inhaled. If she survived, she'd kill Krazy Jay Larkin. But she had Brillo to deal with first.

Lita plucked a used tissue from her pocket, a five-finger discount from aisle ten. She spat on it and wiped her upper lip before dabbing away the crusted blood coating her nostrils. At the beginning of the contest, Brillo surprised her with a backhanded slap. He timed it right, using enough force to allow her to stumble backward without falling.

Lita ran for her life. For a hairy second, she saw her ex-husband's rage flash through Brillo's flat eyes. When her faculties returned, she saw Brillo's immense physique and lamented that her predicament. Brillo's sadistic past didn't offer Lita the luxury of picking at the scabs of her past. He told her there'd be more and that she'd think her bloodied nose a light cracker compared to his other talents.

Anger clouded her memory. Where were the goddamn Doggie Din-Dins? Lita also took a few cans of Roma tomatoes with her. She picked up two cans and filled her lungs with the cold store air.

"Hey Dylan!" she cried out, to resort to her own nickname for him. "Brillo!"

A pin could have shattered the silence within each aisle. Lita needed time to recall the pet food aisle. She reluctantly stepped away from the display. She edged toward the nearest aisle on her right: Pickled vegetables, imported conserves and legumes. No, they couldn't make it so damned easy, she thought and mentally recited her remaining list. Doggie Din-Dins, clothes pegs…five cans of Din Dins no less.

Counting backward, she figured she stood at least eight aisles away from the clothes pegs. The dog food couldn't be far. She'd grab the clothes pegs, sprint toward the checkout, hopefully without encountering Brillo, and be one step closer to freedom.

The holographic screen overhead flickered.

"Lita!" Krazy Jay grinned.

Wretched moron. Lita frowned and looked away from the hologram. She had watched Aisle Madness numerous times to gauge Krazy Jay's strategy. He'd attempt to gauge Krazy Jay's strategy. He'd attempt a conversation at an inconvenient point, usually when the frightened contestant was a hair's breadth away from caressing a much-needed item from the shelf, for the contestant to collide with their unhinged opponent and meet a blood curdling end.

Lita needed to shift a gear.

"I can see you Lita. There is folks, in aisle…"

No please don't say it, but you will say it because you're a cold sadistic bastard who came up with the idea for this show.

Krazy Jay whispered. "Eight."

Lita snapped her head around and inched toward the aisle to her left. If she snuck around, she'd make it to the pet food section and dash toward the wretched yellow and red cans. Doggie Din Dins…the harbinger of her ultimate doom. She covered her mouth and smiled. Karma. Karma for putting their starving dog out of its misery. What kind of society denied pets to its population by making most necessities unattainable? Pets were forbidden to all workers and domiciles. She knew she'd get nowhere with the thought but she clung to her anger.

She spied clothes pegs three feet into the next aisle and sprinted. She needed four packs. She counted five and agonized over her options. In the event of dropping one, she'd have an extra pack.

Brillo yelled. "Darlin' Lita! I miss you!"

Her nostrils flared in response to his voice and her hands shook. She opted for the four packs. Anything more and she'd be weighted down. Lita wiped her damp upper lip. For all she knew, Brillo had the skills of a ventriloquist. She had difficulty fixing his voice to an aisle. As she stood within the aisle, seconds between herself and a sadistic serial murderer, thoughts retreated to the primal corners of her brain. If she stood within aisle eight, she couldn't be far away from the pet food. The handles of the basket slipped against her clammy palm. She tightened her grip.

Brillo continued. "Don't be rude, hon. Don't be mean. Jay's talking to you!"

It couldn't be so easy, Lita thought. Brillo's voice came from her left. She crept toward the middle of the aisle and aimed to exist nearer to the dairy section, turn right and hopefully see aisle seven and dash toward the end, hopefully enter the right aisle to dash toward the checkout and dump her current selection, making room for the dog food.

It had been forever since she'd last visited a supermarket. A jealous coworker sabotages her last job as a shelf refresher. Despite attempts to automate everything, corporations were taken to task when unemployment rose new laws were drafted to maintain a reasonable percentage and despite growing resentment, menial jobs remained. When Lita received the call from Human Services confirming her success, she felt like she had won the national lottery.

Supermarket chains appeared to be in competition, but she suspected it to be closer to monopolistic competition. Most retained similar organizational setups and floor plans, sharing similar special deals and price margins. Lita looked ahead. With her eye fixed on the diary refrigerators in the distance, she raised her right foot and planted it a few inches forward. I can do this, she thought. Her left foot followed.

Brillo screamed. "I can smell you!"

Lita rolled her eyes. And? What else can I do but try?

Confident of her distance, Lita stopped briefly and considered her feet. She had gone with Jet's suggestion and wore her vintage Converse sneakers for luck. Smiling at the irony, she continued her brisk walk, reaching the end of the aisle with her breath stuffed within her chest. She turned her head instinctively to the left. Chest straining, she raised her right hand to her mouth to muffle the slightest hint of life. She inhaled slowly and blinked away the floaters. With a swift turn of her head, she spied the distant fresh produce.

Melons.

Her list automatically flashed in her mind.

3 x Melons.

5 x Doggie Din Dins.

Racing to the display, basket swinging, she hoisted three melons, twisted her head round as a precautionary measure, to see Brillo calmly stride down the aisle. Time not only slowed, it coalesced into a gelatinous mess that felt as though it had settled in her knees.

"No you don't," she muttered, hugging the three melons. She sprinted to the first available checkout and dumped the melons and clothes pegs. Then the lights flickered.

ZZZ…zzz…ffft….ft…szzz…

Lita looked up while her ears operated on autopilot, monitoring Brillo's oddly gentle footfalls on the polished floor. Dread congregated like a swarm of hornets within her gut. She expected Krazy Jay's holographic form to spring up in front of her. in her rush, she missed the pet food aisle.

Brillo called out. "There's nowhere to run sweetie! You sure have a pretty behind.

But you already know that don't you? I bet you get complimented all the time. Think you're something…"

For his voice to be audible, he had to be nearer. Lita turned and walked, hoping to collide with a food display. She wondered about the purpose of food displays in a world where only the exclusive few afforded to shop freely. A world where a can of peeled tomatoes cost more than twenty dollars.

I'm something, Lita thought. I'm goddamn terrified and motivated. Talk about containing two conflicting ideas in my head. Need to run away now. Need to win. Terrified all round.

Sweat trickled to the small of her back like a praying mantis. From her periphery she spied the Hershey's and realised that she had missed the pet food section.

"Damn! Damn you Brillo!" she screamed, turning on her heel and briefly stopping, to see her opponent a good distance away. "You're deranged. You're hideous. You think I'm scared?" Lita narrowed her eyes. "You're right, there is nowhere to run. I have nothing else to lose."

Brillo stopped and presented her with a maniacal grin that accentuated his triangular goatee.

"Love the triangle of fur Brillo. Does it turn the girls on? You look like you've grown a vagina on your chin!"

Her boldness briefly dazzled him. She took her chance and dashed toward the chocolate, picking up more than two bars. She stuffed them in her pockets and sprinted up the aisle, turned right, pulled off her shoes and dashed to the pet food aisle, to come to a slow stop.

"I can smell you, bitch!"

Sure you can, she thought. Lita braced for difficulty. There were no baskets nearby to accommodate the canned dog food. Who could afford a pet? Her inner voice offered a swift reply: The wretched cream of the social crop. The zero point zero, zero, zero fucking zero nine percent. At 15 dollars per can, the life of a dog was a charmed one. Dogs were the new It Bag, exceeding the price tag of a Birkin. The dog she had to euthanize was worthless. What the Human Services Department categorized a "Bitzer", a mixed breed that had no value due to its genetic hybridity.

She evaluated the Doggie Din Dins and smiled. There was no such thing as a larger variety; shoppers paid for one size or had to forgo the product. Transporting the cans was as simple as one embrace. Three under one arm, two in the other. Lita visually rehearsed her maneuver; she'd drop the cans on the checkout counter, drop the two Hershey bars and press the verification button.

In the distance, Brillo grumbled. "You're no fun! I'll complain to the fat cat at the top of this stupid program!"

Lita blanked out, guessing his new strategy involving a form of ventriloquism. His perversity didn't surprise. According to his gravel voice, he had to have been standing two aisles away. She moved forward and picked up her barefooted pace, counting steps in her head: One, two, three, four, not much to go, five, six, seven, almost three, eight…

"But I want you now!" Brillo called.

Without a moment to spare, Lita sprinted toward the checkout and dropped the cans. Turning she saw Brillo launch his solid body forward. She fumbled for the chocolate, swallowed anxiety and fear and tossed the two bars at the checkout counter. With a short hop, she almost tumbled forward on her ankle, her eye on the hulking killer when the lights flickered.

Zzzzz-fttt-szzzzz.

Darkness interrupted Brillo's deranged notion of a rendezvous. Lita used her palms to push herself up like a sprinter preparing for the starter gun.

"Careful you don't crash into a wall or me."

Lita willed her eyes to adjust to the opacity of the supermarket. Humans were always at a disadvantage. How many more centuries would pass for further devolution? Her high school biology teacher's speech returned to mind: Humans have been evolving over time but since we don't have as many predators as, let's say…a cat, we don't need to see in the dark. Lame, she thought. It didn't offer her a solution to her blind sprint.

Zssss…zzzz….ftttt…ft…

"Come on!" Lita sniped. The lights flickered repeatedly, mucking up her visual focus. Brillo's calm footsteps echoed down the aisle, as did his incessant hum. The honking monotone aggravated her doubts like a light switch being flicked up and down repeatedly. Her thigh muscles twitched as she turned into the unseen aisle.

Brillo continued his solid pace.

"I have some trivial for you. Feline predators like tigers don't roar before they strike, oh no. Do you know the sound they make, dear Lita?"

Lita kept walking. She kept herself to one side of the aisle, careful to keep the fingers of her left hand a short distance away from the products lest she dropped a jar, crinkled cellophane or bumped plastic. She didn't underestimate Brillo's honed sense of sound; he had built up a horrendous reputation as a stalker, preferring to tranquilize his female quarry, dump them in nearby forests and spend hours stalking them until they, after hours without water or food, collapsed begging for mercy that evolved into a grisly torture session.

She felt cornered and her breath came forth in short bursts. You don't dupe me with trivia questions, she thought.

"Tigers make a strange noise before their attack. It's a clicking sound." Brillo clucked his tongue to imitate the sound. "And they don't attack from the front my darling. No they don't."

Lita's sweat poured into her mouth. She stopped and pondered the opacity of the aisle. There is no dairy aisle here, stupid. There is nothing. It had been a while between supermarkets. Even her time as a shelf refresher was restricted to daylight hours. She had never been inside a supermarket in complete darkness.

ZZsssz….ztzzzz…zzzzZzzzzsssff….ssssz.

"They strike from BEHIND!"

Her mouth fell open. Lita's feet left the floor. Lights blinked on, off, on, off and Lita couldn't scream due to the burly arm squeezing her windpipe. She kicked her feet and tried swallowing, for tears to well in her eyes. The warm trail of Brillo's tongue against her neck almost drained her.

"Whazzamatter? Don't like that? That's what you all say." His voice rose in pitch, blasted her eardrum. "You don't like this; you don't like that. Not tonight, not in the mood…"

For once Lita found a useful item handing between the sauces. The sections between shelves contained useless items, distractions for shoppers such as egg slicers, bottle caps and, what offered her hope, bottle openers. Lita lurched forward a couple of times, using her momentum to throw her hand forward.

Please…

Please…be easy to grab.

Brillo alternated between high and low pressure, playing a perverted breath game. Lita's gulp for air, interrupted within sections, provided sufficient morsels of air to keep her from passing out and entering Brillo's symbolic intimate play zone. Three attempts with her hand, feet kicking all the while, she unhooked the pack and tore the package open with her teeth, taking any chance she could, and pulled the bottle opener, tasting blood as her lateral incisor felt out of her mouth.

"Feisty. I like that word. You're a firecracker all right." He squeezed a little harder, forcing the air out of her. She deflated like an accordion and, tightly clutching the opener, launched the pointed end upward until he dropped her abruptly.

His scream echoed through the aisle and whistled through to her eardrum. She spat out more blood and put her hand against her ear. "Agghughhh," she mumbled, as an auditory test. She retreated, bottle opener in hand, to stumble backward over a fallen can.

"That's how I like it, honey. When you're on your back, you're all mine." Brillo still held his hand over his bloody eye and displayed a symmetrical row of yellowed teeth through his menacing grin.

Lita quickly gripped the can, glimpsed its contents and couldn't feel more ridiculous. The bottle opener was useless from the distance. Its short point wouldn't remain lodged in Brillo's flesh.

"Hey, bastard. Care for spaghetti sauce?"

Anxiety coiled with fear until her adrenaline migrated to her core, rendering her limbs partially numb. The can flew upward, its metallic ridge slammed against Brillo's forehead, sending him into a brief daze.

Zzzzz…zzz…sst…zzzzz…ssssfzzzz.

The lights stopped flickering. Lita blinked and gripped a second can as she slowly rose on her feet. "And that."

Brillo's other hand shot to his nose. "You petty bitch!" He roared something unintelligible and took a long stride forward.

Lita didn't view herself as a reality shopper or competitor. The state assigned and regulated occupational roles and economic sectors. To be selected for a role with a potentially lucrative outcome, for the term of her natural life, as well as that of her son's, couldn't be ignored or treated as an ethical issue. She visualised a baseball pitch and launched a third can, followed by a fourth and fifth; Brillo's nose bled profusely. He pulled away his bearish hand and frowned. His mouth then fell open.

"Wh-ah?"

"And that," she aimed a sixth that hit him square in the mouth, loosening his front teeth. Lita went to town, recalling the ping-pong carnie clowns. Suddenly she craved to see her handiwork, knock out the remaining teeth in his head.

A seventh can dislodged his front teeth. "And that's for the poor girls you mutilated, you freak!"

Brillo rubbed his mouth and swaggered as he viewed both bloody hands.

"T…T…"

"And we are back! The network apologizes for the technical issues but we are back and boy have we missed a doozie of a match! Brillo, bloody and battered by…What's that?" Krazy Jay paused. Lita didn't bite, kept aiming can after can.

"Lita you've been a very bad girl, haven't you?" Eleven…twelve…thirteen…fourteen… Brillo swayed like a wounded serpent.

"I want out of here. I want out now!" She yelled at Jay. "I've satisfied the conditions."

"But you haven't completed the game," Jay said sweetly. "Audience, please remind Lita about the rules of the game."

The audience complied and chanted.

"Kill! Kill! Kill!"

"According to our current monitor, Dylan is still alive. Yes, when you registered, we did send a complimentary chocolate beverage. Did you drink that Lita?"

Lita nodded slowly and poked out her head to check on Brillo. The burly killer lay flat on the polished floor, a small pool of his blood coagulated over his lower lip.

"That beverage contained a small device. A nano-molecule and that little machine is still in your. Our friend Brillo has an identical device. That device monitors the vital signs and although Dylan may appear to be dead, his vital signs say otherwise. So, you see, you haven't satisfied all the required conditions."

He adopted the monotone of the employment bureau. Contractual obligations. Small print. Disclaimers.

"The longer you take, the higher your vulnerability. Because I'm tellin' you babay, when Dylan gets up, he'll be one bat crazed mother…Whoa!" Jay put his hand over his mouth. "I forgot! We have your son here Lita. I'm sorry, my boy."

Jet frowned. "C'mon Mom. What's taking so long?"

Lita shook her head. "I'm trying. I'm trying!" She blinked away from the screen.

Jet's voice rose. "You have to do it Mom. It's not that hard. Go on," he implored.

What are you people doing to children? While she couldn't consider her son apathetic and violent, now as she stood half bloody and battered, she duly noted her absences. Parents toiled for hours, sometimes juggling three jobs to provide the bare minimum as children were left to their own devices, seated in front of virtual machines, engaging in who knew what and where, with strangers. Killers even.

Krazy Jay dominated the view. "What's it going to be? We have all night. Our sponsors are so excited to add extra advertising slots. If you do win, you'll also have a breakfast cereal named after you."

"What will it be called moron? Lita Bran?"

"It can be anything you want." He raised a perfectly groomed brow. "That is if you can manage to finish him off."

"He is finished," she said. From her location, she noted his slightly misshapen forehead. "His head has taken so many cans. I'm betting he's braindead."

"Superficial swelling of the skin. That's nothing. He is quiet well indeed," Jay said. The audience recommenced chanting.

The screen switched to a grid that displayed two sets of vital signs. Lita considered finality, didn't like it one iota. She had spent far too many hours eluding a serial killer within an eerily quiet supermarket and managed to complete her irrelevant shopping list, to be given a final condition. It's how they suck you in, Lita. All multinationals do it. If it's not thirty day interest free finance, it's high purchase.

She walked over to Brillo and stood at his feet, careful to avoid his hands. He breathed slowly, confirming his reasonable health.

"What will it be?" Jays voice echoed.

Lita swallowed, reached for a can and contemplated the transition from ordinary drone mom to reality network killer contestant. She'd be considered a champion and there were only two other reigning champions. But her son's eagerness and apathy niggled her. They did get to him, like they get to all kids. They began with pretty commercials targeted at toddlers. Smiling cereal, talking cookies and animated toys promised a world of fun. As the children shifted from toddlerhood into childhood, they brought out the heavy duty action figures. Boys were tough, with high tech laser pistols. Girls still used toy household gadgets. Things rarely change.

Sighing, Lita looked at Brillo's face and considered the most repellant question. Could her son evolve into a Brillo?

The slight flutter of Brillo's eyelids paralyzed Lita's thoughts and, along with those, her hand. The can rolled away from Brillo.

Lita fell. Pressure gripped her ankle. Brillo had been too quick, hastening her decision as she came down over him, her knee slammed down hard against his neck. She thought she heard something crunch. His eyelids fluttered forward like an antique porcelain doll.

As she knelt, an ongoing sound thrashed against her ears. The sound rose.

Bleeeeeep…

"We have our champion folks!"

"Wha?" Lita blinked at Brillo, expecting his brutal resurrection.

"You're the winner. A lifetime's supply of groceries for you and your
family, in your case your son Jet who is leaping for joy here. Come here, Jet. Congratulate your mother!" Jay roared like a sportscaster.

"I've done it?"

Jay yelled. "You've done it! You've won." His mouth gaped. "Mommy!"

Lita grimaced as she stood, her knees creaking on the way up. She moved forward.

"But…"

"Mom!"

Oblivious to the monitor, Lita made a quick mental shopping list. It had been a near decade since she ate a red apple. Her body cried out for apples, chocolate chip cookies, and real cow's milk instead of the powdered soy substitute.

"Mommmm!"

Lita smiled to herself. She didn't do too badly. She beat them. She beat the transnational ghouls and took down a serial killer to boot.

"Mom! Mom!"

"What is it, Jet?" Lita looked up at the holographic screen, unaware of the slow but certain twitch behind her until her face met the polished floor. Lita tasted salt and iron and felt the fingers in her left hand crack like peanut shells. A thunderous flash clanged inside her head like the world's largest gong.

"A..oo…wiar…"

"What's that, darl? You're calling me a liar? Tsk-tsk. Well that makes me a wounded host!" Jay snarled.

Krazy Jay came into view as Brillo lodged a stainless-steel bottle opener into Lita's spine.

"There. I've got you now," Brillo whispered, smiling at the holograph. He threw away the stacked cylinder of plastic cups responsible for the crack that Lita presumed to be his neck.

"Aw...No! My goodness! It seems like our equipment malfunctioned again.

Technology isn't always smooth or perfect, I'm afraid," he said, followed by canned oos and ahhs. "It's such a shame. She was so close. Never mind! What do you say to a consolation prize, Jet? A lifetime contract with Transfood Global, the official sponsor of Aisle Madness?"

"Do I get food?"

"Jet, as a consolation prize winner you receive a lifetime contract as a minor shareholder. As a shareholder, you receive out of date products to utilize as you wish. When you finish school, you'll work and have two days vacation a year, for as long as you wish to work." Jay smiled at the audience. "Of course, there are few alternatives but to work. All this brought to you by Wocol!

Jet grinned at the camera and shrugged. "I'll do it. Yeah. Excecool." The final word, an amalgamation of excellent and cool was lost on Krazy Jay.

"Wave goodbye Jet."

"Bye everyone."

Jay's porcelain teeth dominated the camera, but his entire form materialised within all tuned homes.

"Don't forget next week. We will have a new winner...or loser..." More canned elation and laughter seeped into the market as Lita's final taunt. Despite using her arms to crawl forward, Brillo's firm grip on her ankles kept her lower body from slumping onto the ground. Her brain screamed instructions but the spinal bottle opener

scrambled all the signals to her legs.

"Please," she said hoarsely.

"Hasn't this life taught you anything Lita? You can't have everything. Not when you're born in the cheap seats."

The holographs vanished and Brillo pulled Lita away, leaving a trail of tears and saliva behind as reminders of her life, which would only last until the arrival of the cleaners.

The End.

Case #90751

Anastasia

Anastasia strives to balance creative writing with her postgraduate law studies. Due to study demands, The Cheap Seats is the first full length short story that she has had published for a while. Her love of horror took root in childhood, sneaking out of her bed to watch her childhood horror idols Vincent Price, Peter Cushing and Christopher Lee on television, and she has never looked back. Details of her current and future work will be updated on her shiny new blog: http://readerdiscretionisadvised.wordpress.com

Fish

Luke Tarzian

ALLAN IS A COOK. ACTUALLY, HE USED TO BE A COOK: but he was fired. Nothing major; Allan plunged a knife into the right arm of a patron several times. What else was he supposed to do? The fat man said his steak was terrible; smelt like shit and tasted like a horse's cock. And that's absolutely unacceptable. He also told the blob to cut the fat off of his ass and fry it in a pan. Maybe that would sate his everlasting hunger.

Fat fuck.

Allan went to prison for a while for attempted murder (it was really self-defense, he argued) and attended weekly sessions with psychiatrists. Don't be so quick to jump the gun, they told him as they scribbled on their boards. Don't let the cruelty of another rule your actions. Otherwise, the cycle never ends.

The cycle never even started for that tub of lard, says Allan every time. You'd agree with me if you had seen him. Fuck, he probably would have bent the bicycle....

I see, say the psychiatrists, still scribbling as if their lives depended on that line of scratch. Intolerant. Volatile....

Allan is released a few years later. No restaurant will hire him; the episode is quite familiar to many, so he finds a writing job; clerical; they deal with food: tasting and critiquing. Allan wants to be a critic, but his bosses tell him no: he'll start out pushing papers, punching numbers, writing letters—then, perhaps, they'll reconsider.

And so Allan goes about his work begrudgingly, grumbling to himself until it's time to clock out and go home. Home: his shabby little piece of heaven with a kitchen fully stocked and waiting to birth something new and wonderful. Allan's been all over, tasted nearly every kind of steak, every kind of meat: they're all intriguing to him, have their own distinctive tastes...yet they lack excitement, lack that certain zing that really pumps the blood and makes a man exclaim, "God fucking dammit, this is what I call a steak!" And that's what Allan wants to find—that certain zing. It isn't garlic, nor is it paprika (don't ask why people put this crap on steak; Allan is completely clueless on the matter), and it sure as hell is not that "secret sauce" some fast food restaurants put in their meat (that, as far as Allan is concerned, is horse piss filtered through a dusty tube). Maybe it's not the seasoning; maybe it's the meat....

Allan scrapes his current dish into the trash, pondering.

Maybe it's the meat.

He'll find that zing.

***

The Boiler.

Allan's never been here. It's a seedy looking place beside the docks, but it's the only place he can afford to eat at, having just paid rent. He steps into the building and it's dark and musty, but Allan doesn't care. He sits down at a table, waiting to be served. He looks around the room: several dirty men sit scattered, drinking solitary in the corners. They must see too much of one another on the docks, thinks Allan as the waiter greets him with a jagged, yellow smile.

"Interested in the special? Only ten bucks for the first-time customer," says the waiter.

Allan nods.

"Sure."

The waiter nods, still grinning down at Allan.

"Coming up! I'll make sure they cook it extra special." He winks at Allan and disappears into the kitchen, apron swinging with each step.

The waiter steps out thirty minutes later with a steaming plate of meat. It's dark brown, nearly black in several areas, but somehow smells delicious. Allan cuts the edge, stabs it with his fork, and shoves the food into his mouth, savoring its tenderness, salivating at its juiciness.

"Fantastic, eh?" the waiter says, nudging Allan with a smirk.

Fantastic.

"Superb," Allan marvels. "I've…never tasted something so divine, so succulent and tender…not even veal…."

The waiter leans in close and whispers in his ear, "The secret's in the whipping; age is key as well."

Allan cocks his head.

"The animal…what is it? What part am I eating?"

The waiter grins, flashing yellowed teeth. "Man ass."

57

Allan nearly chokes.

"Come again?"

The waiter merely smiles, pats Allan on the shoulder, and departs. Allan sits a moment, frozen by the words—man ass. Is it true?

Has he really eaten human flesh? Is he content with knowing such a thing? He takes another bite, chewing thoughtfully.

Fuck it.

He devours it.

***

Allan does not step into restaurant again. Two weeks pass before he even ponders doing so. He's tried to fight the longing—it's not natural, he knows—but it's far too strong; it has that zing. The yearning for the meat deprives him of his sleep; the constant hunger draws his focus and he falls behind his tasks at work. He wants another taste; needs another taste—he's desperate for the tender treat.

Allan ventures towards the restaurant one day for lunch, tingling with anticipation. He turns the corner—his heart drops. The restaurant, the keeper of his drug...it isn't there; nothing is there. It's all been demolished.

Allan smacks his lips; he's shaking now, shivering. He's desperate. He heads back to the office, clocks out early, says he's sick, and treks several blocks to some steakhouse: he needs meat; his hunger must be sated. He orders chicken; beef; turkey; duck; alligator; every fucking piece of meat the menu has to offer—they do not serve his needs; they do not quench. He skips out on the check; he cannot possibly afford the bill. Allan slips into the evening, itching, hungry....

People eye him oddly as he heads for home. His arms are wrapped around his body like he's shivering—because he's shivering—and he's mumbling to himself, eyes darting to and fro as if hallucinating, as if he's leery, paranoid.... He needs an option: some way to procure

that which he so desperately desires. He begins to eye the other passersby; but they all look too strong, and most are travelling in pairs. His head twitches as he tries to shake away the thoughts. That is not the proper thing to do.

He shuffles into his apartment complex, stumbles up the stairs and walks the hallway towards his dingy room. He stops several feet from his door. Something haggard sits beside the foot mat, something young and dirty, blonde(ish), blue-eyed, weary and bleeding. Allan nears it cautiously: it's just a girl, no more than ten, homeless. The thought returns; he glances to and fro: there's no one near. He reaches towards the girl, smiling.

"Come here, sweetheart; let's fix you up a bit."

***

They're in the living room now. Allan's standing nervously beside the front door as the blonde girl sits down on the floor. He's hesitant, but the hunger will not leave. He itches everywhere; his vision's slightly blurred. His stomach growls—hurry up. Allan bolts the door and heads into the bathroom.

"I'll be back in just a minute, sweetheart. Then we'll fix you up a bit."

He studies his reflection. This might be a little messy; he has work tomorrow. He takes off his clothing; now he's naked, staring at his scrawny reflection. He cracks his neck and steps back into the living room. The girl takes notice, stands up, and makes for the door. She's too slow.

"Come here, sweetheart. Now let's fix you up a bit."

He throws himself upon her, knocks her to the floor. His naked body pins her to the rug. She tries to scream; he chokes her—one hand on her tiny throat, the other covering her mouth and nose. The process is exhilarating; the waiter's words resound inside his head— the whipping. He begins to smack her, soft at first, then harder, alternating areas of interest: thighs; calves; forearms; stomach; cheeks; buttocks.

She's not breathing anymore. Allan looks down; he hadn't noticed how excited he's become. He's made a mess. He shrugs; he'll clean it later—right now he is starving. He steps into the bathroom, runs a hot bath till the tub is halfway full, steaming, and retrieves the body—"Let's fix you up a bit, sweetheart"—, dumping it into the water, watching as the locks of blonde hair float like seaweed in the ocean: peacefully. Allan steps into the kitchen, grasps his meat saw in his hand, and returns to carve his steak. He pauses for a moment, considering what he has and is about to do. She's homeless: no one will miss her.

So he carves and cuts, rends and tears; drains the tub and fills it up again. Several hours pass; the process is repeated many times until he has procured the cuts he wants. He carries them into the kitchen, starts the stove, and goes to work, seasoning and adding salt where it is needed. It's nearly one a.m. when Allan's cooking is complete. He takes a fork and knife, cuts the meat, and prays. He takes a bite; chewing slowly…slower…he swallows and lets out a sigh of ecstasy.

It's perfect.

***

It's Tuesday, the 30th of May in 1978; Allan's sitting in a waiting room in Mexico, humming to himself; a happy little tune he's just come up with. The television's on—it's the news. A mother's weeping, a father's pleading: little Gwenlin Buck has now been missing for two days. She's ten years old, blonde hair, dark blue eyes, last seen at the park. Her parents think she might have wandered off. Always an adventurer they say. Allan smirks.

"Oh dear…."

He licks his lips.

A dark-haired woman steps into the waiting room to greet him. They shake hands; her name is Mary.

"Welcome to the orphanage, señor," she says, leading Allan down a corridor. He can hear their laughter in the walls, echoing. Mary smiles up at him. "It's such a great thing, adoption. How long have you been considering, Mister…um…I'm so sorry. We spoke yesterday on the phone, but your name seems to have slipped my mind."

Allan smiles.

"No need to worry," he says kindly. "Just a couple days now, actually. And it's Allan—Allan Fish."

The End.

Case #78841
Luke Tarzian

Luke was born in Bucharest, Romania in 1990 and has been writing since 2005. He's a graduate of the California State University of Fullerton, with a B.A. in English. He's an aspiring novelist, a lover of cats, and likes to indulge in a nice Jack and Coke every now and then. He firmly believes that Grumpy Cat is his soul animal. His favorite writers are Edgar Allan Poe and Neil Gaiman, and he is currently working on the second and third books in his *"Sewn From Seeds"* trilogy. His work has appeared in several issues of Sanitarium Magazine and his Dracula origin story, *Durante Lucus*, was recently sold to Alban Lake's *Blood Bond* imprint.

Luketarzian.wordpress.com
Facebook.com/rowesofficial
Twitter.com/luke_tarzian

CLAYTON HILL SANITARIUM

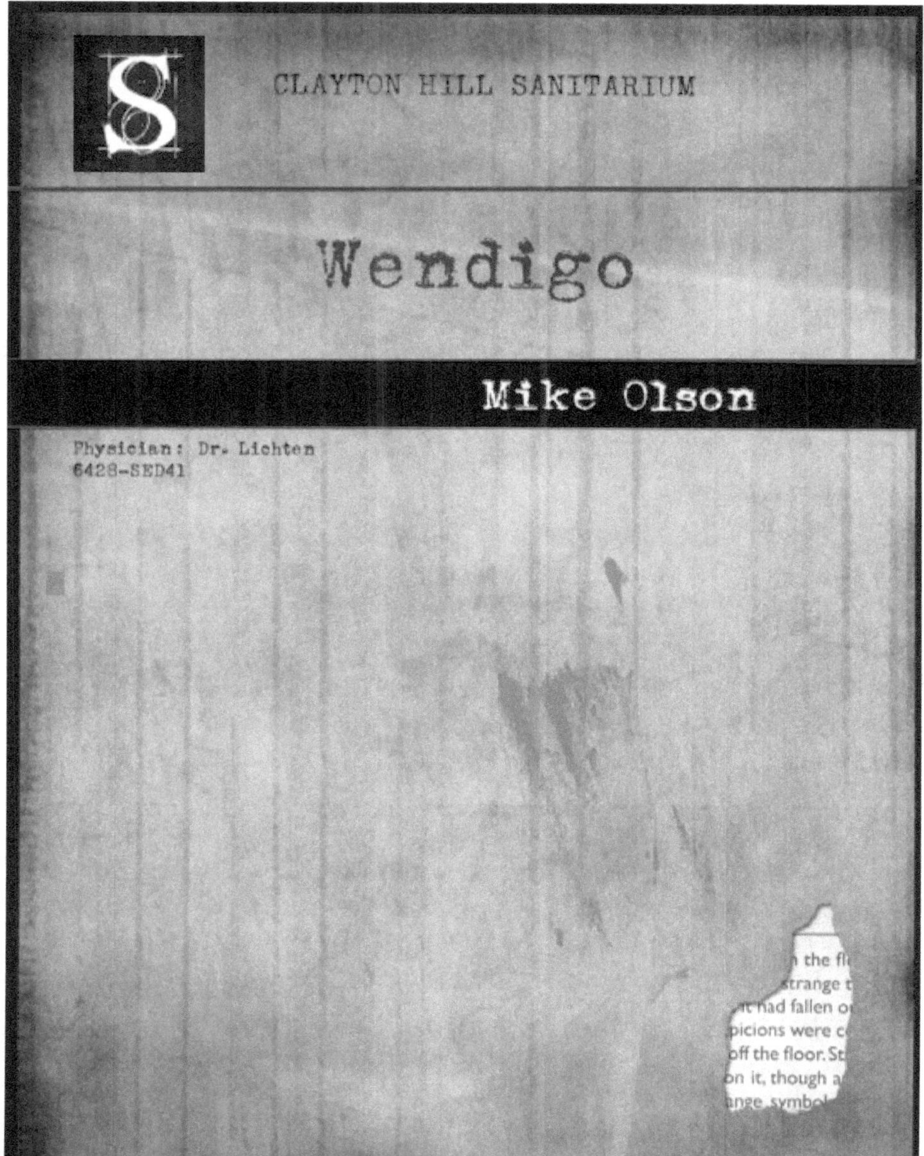

Wendigo

Mike Olson

Physician: Dr. Lichten
6428-SED41

THE MUSINGS OF ONE WHOM, having run out of gas in the South-eastern Appalachians faces the promise of an interminable walk and the prospect of spending the night alongside a lonesome mountain highway.

How a setting sun has changed Chestnut Mountain…

The air is too thin here; my lungs protest, portend a need for every bit of oxygen. A cool gust, a spectral touch or phantom breath, chilling to the very marrow. The sallow traces of necrotic sun bleed between prison bars of White Ash and Yellow Birch, and the graven silence of the woods hammers my ears like raging titans. Faster and ever faster down a damned desolate drag of highway and I supplicate what gods may be for a car, a motorcycle, a hitchhiker to keep me company. Darkness germinates like kudzu, and coupled with stillness paints a grim Van Gough penetrated by my lonely flashlight.

My thoughts race with eidolon of Jungian daemons, childhood ghouls; the machinations of King, the ghost of Lovecraft. What absurdities. No more witchcraft in the moon then a moon in the sky, and god, the inkiness is so complete.

Silence.

Stillness.

Darkness.

Cold.

These are the trappings of the mountain at night…

And the smell of pine, underneath that, the scent of a wolf.

I've never smelled a wolf, but one can imagine. Like a wet dog and stale blood. The hot breath of carnage on a frigid breeze, a slaughterhouse in the dead of winter. My mind plays tricks, wolves hunt in packs, they howl and they snarl and gnash their teeth and run and oh God I'm running. I know I smell death that I cannot see and I cannot hear. The road betrays me. The hammer of my shoes on blacktop. I take to the unfathomed wild. God help me.

Birch rush past me unseen until upon me; I cannot risk dousing my light though I may cover the breadth of its brilliance, for the threat of calamity lives both in beast and precipice. I slow. Something inside me says the wolf is counterfeit; no two legs may outrun four I should be dead were there a predator. Laughter. Laughter like you've never heard before. If no one is around to hear it yes it still makes a sound. Perhaps I scented a dead coyote or fox. Now to liberate the blaze and find the road.

The stark luminescence contrasts so sharply the abyssal gloom as to be momentarily blinding and it reveals a face unreal and unthinkably close by. Eyes milky and cataractal and a vacuous olfactory hole. Gristly locks tumbling over misshapen, blasphemous features around a mouth at once too large for the countenance and too small for the teeth. A horror from some primeval memory of my cave-ancestors spews forth from the depths of my bowels my blood pounds in my temples; madness threatens the edges of my conscious mind and I run.

Trees strike me, ferns trip me, the smell - oh God the smell of blood, bile and all things dead and unholy. And that face is right behind me, there is no pace fast enough, no distance far enough I can traverse to escape that awful mouth, longer my stride harder my breath. I must run harder; my heart fills my ears as that image my eyes my shoes meet the soft resistance of forest floor, tripping roots, a ledge and I think I am falling but panic overcomes...

No light now.

No light and no sound.

***

No more running and no more falling. A coolness against my skin perhaps. Listless. No sleep though, no sleep and no light. Just smell. And faint, maybe miles away, a soft tearing. A child tugging at the legs of a favored teddy. Just a soft sound and a new smell. Iron, or maybe copper. So strong and so nearby, the constant ripping sound so distant. So quiet. The coolness on my face. No light now. No light and no sound...

The End.

Case #64241

Mike Olson

Details not released
at this time.

CLAYTON HILL SANITARIUM

Bestselling Horror US

1 The Line (Witching Savannah, Book One) - *J. D. Horn*

2   The Walk - *Lee Goldberg*

3   Broken Visions (Shattered Promises, #3) - *Jessica Sorensen*

4   Doctor Sleep: A Novel - *Stephen King*

5   11/22/63 - *Stephen King*

6   Pines (The Wayward Pines Series) - *Blake Crouch*

7   This is the End: The Post-Apocalyptic Set - *J. Thorn*

8   The Bird Eater - *Ania Ahlborn*

9   The Stones of Angkor - *Sam Sisavath*

10   The Shining - *Stephen King*

Compiled April 1st -April 31st 2014
Amazon.com Kindle Chart

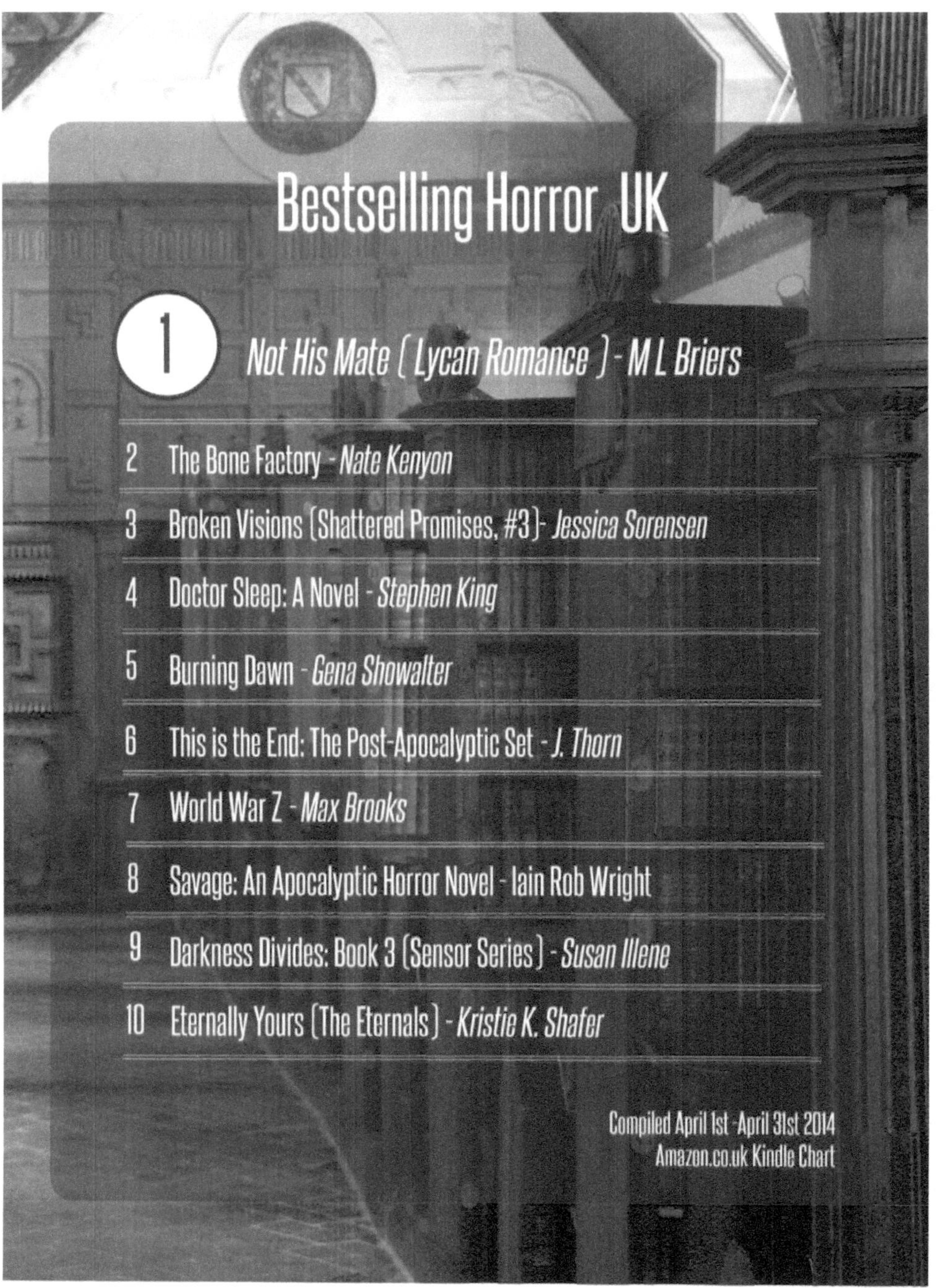

Bestselling Horror UK

1 *Not His Mate (Lycan Romance) - M L Briers*

2   The Bone Factory - *Nate Kenyon*

3   Broken Visions (Shattered Promises, #3)- *Jessica Sorensen*

4   Doctor Sleep: A Novel - *Stephen King*

5   Burning Dawn - *Gena Showalter*

6   This is the End: The Post-Apocalyptic Set - *J. Thorn*

7   World War Z - *Max Brooks*

8   Savage: An Apocalyptic Horror Novel - Iain Rob Wright

9   Darkness Divides: Book 3 (Sensor Series) - *Susan Illene*

10   Eternally Yours (The Eternals) - *Kristie K. Shafer*

Compiled April 1st -April 31st 2014
Amazon.co.uk Kindle Chart

Group
Therapy
05.14
Horror Writers Association
Awards Winners 2013

The Horror Writers Association Awards (HWA) is a global, non-profit organization of writers and publishers who are dedicated to promotion writings of horror and dark literature. The association was formed in 1985m with the help of Dean Koontz, Joe R. Lansdale and Robert McCammon. HWA was formally incorporated in the year 1987 and that was the first year when it gave out the Bram Stoker Awards.

The Bram Stoker Awards are recognitions given by the Horrors Writers Association for achievements in dark literature and horror writing. The awards are named after the Irish horror writer, Bram Stoker, known famously for his novel, Dracula. The winners are selected by votes of the active members of the association and are awarded amongst the following active categories currently:

- First novel
- Novel
- Young, adult novel,
- Long fiction
- Short fiction
- Graphic novel
- Fiction collection
- Non-fiction
- Anthology
- Screen play
- Poetry collection
- Lifetime Achievement

The award ceremony for the year 2014 was held at the World Horror Convention 2014 in Portland, Oregon. This year, the HWA chose two of the best long-time icons of the dark genre to receive the prestigious award of Lifetime Achievement, Stephen Jones and R.L. Stine.

Stephen Jones is a renowned name in the world of horror writing and dark literature. His works throughout have received recognition in the form of awards from World Fantasy Awards, international Horror Guild Awards, HWA Bram Stoker Awards,

British Fantasy Awards and has also received a Hugo Award nominee too.

R L. Stine has been one of the best-selling horror and fictional writers for children. His Goosebumps series have sold over 300 million copies in US alone and along with that, he is one of the best and top publishing phenomenon for more than 32 languages in all. His stories, anthology TV series-horror, feature films and a lot of other works in the genre, contributed immensely to the field of dark literature and earned him the lifetime achievement award at the HWA Bram Stoker Awards 2014.

The Lifetime Achievement Award has been the most prestigious award at the HWA Bram Stoker Awards. It is given as an acknowledgement of achievement of superior work not only once but throughout an entire career of the professional. Recipients of the award are chosen by a special committee annually and include writers and professionals who have exhibited profound contributions to the field and are at least over sixty years of age and have also published for a minimum period of 35 years.

The list of Bram Stoker Awards for this year, along with their winners is as follows:

Stephen King won the award for Superior Achievement in a Novel for his novel Doctor Sleep (The Shining #2). This time Stephen King returned to the characters and time span of his popular novel, The Shining, and brought about this insanely riveting novel which got him the Bam Stoker Awards 2014.

Rocky Wood bagged away the award for Superior Achievement in a Graphic novel for his work in Witch Hunts: A Graphic History of Burning Times in 2012. The novel talked about the witch hunters and their execution methods, trials and tortures of the arrested witches. This novel was set about three centuries back in the era when Black Death rampaged Europe. This year the same category was won over by Caitlin R. Kiernan for Alabaster Wolves.

Superior achievement in a Fiction Collection was won by Laird Baron's The Beautiful Thing That Awaits Us All and Other Stories published by Night Shade Books. Superior achievement in short fiction was won by Night Train to Paris, written by David Gerrold and published by The Magazine of Fantasy and Science Fiction, ed. Jan/Feb 2013.

Superior achievement in an Anthology was bagged by After Death, edited by Eric J. Guingard and published by Dark Moon Books. The award for superior achievement in Screenplay was won by The Walking Dead: Welcome to the Tombs by Glen MAzzara and which was aired on AMC TV.

All in all, the HWA Bram Stoker Awards 2013 were a glam event and included a number of successful winners from the past and some new potential names introduced in the world of dark literature this year.

Fancy going to next years gala event?

Head over to horror.org for more information on how to join the

HWA.

Sandor

Joad Nacer

Physician: Dr. Peterson
9268-WCT29

I AM WRITING THIS STORY IN AN asylum in rural london, hoping that it will be published not as a tale of fiction but as an article exploring the eldritch life that we cannot and do not want to see, the autobiography of a scientist who lost his sanity upon being confronted with a terror of unimaginable horror. However, I doubt that this story will ever leave the confines of my small cell, and if it does it does then I imagine that it will only be published as the delusional ramblings of an eccentric southern bourgeois.

It was in the summer of 1879 that I was informed of my grandfather's demise. My parents having died a few years ago, both from unknown causes, making me the heir to my grandfather's estate. The estate had been built almost a millennium ago and had been passed down from De Locke to De Locke. Only once before had the estate been in the possession of someone not named De Locke, when the Duke of Edinburgh gifted it to Lord Duncan, a lowly farm owner who had risen far beyond his rank a feat shrouded in mystery. This would be the second time that someone named anything other than De Locke would own the castle, for my mother was the one carrying the name, and I naturally took my father's, Sandor.

I feel that before we may continue, it is important that I take a moment to speak about myself. I come from an old and well-respected southern family, and have always thought of myself as being superior to others. I was home schooled by my father's tutor, and thanks to his teachings I was able to conduct successful research in the fields of astronomy and astrology, discovering a star that I believe controls what most people know as luck. Of course, looking into such divine matters leaves a mark on any mortal mind, and so I find myself often worrying about the smallest of things. While on a pleasant walk through the nearby countryside, it is not uncommon for me to break into a run, convinced that I am being followed. I keep a diary upon my body at all times, and I write all of my fears and suspicions into it. In this diary, I also keep records on the people around me, which includes a brief description of their personality, family tree and a sketch of their visage. I also note

down anything they do that I believe could be important, such as debts they owe,
people they dislike and various trivial nonsense that I really shouldn't bother with. Why I do this, even I ignore.

Four days after receiving the news of my grandfather's death, I set off for the estate. It took me a day to get there, during which I reflected upon my newfound wealth. I would lie if I said that I was sad about his passing; even though I did know him, I never thought much of him. He was, as is of all rich old men, eccentric. Whenever I would dine with him, he would quickly descend into incoherent ramblings about ghosts and fate, and a vast portion of the family was sure that he indulged in the occasional pagan ritual. His wealth however, was never a cause of any problem – wealth never is. While he lacked money, he had a vault filled with antiques, tapestries, statues and relics. He also possessed a 24 carat pink diamond that was estimated to be worth three hundred thousand pounds. We had tried to get him to sell it on many occasions, but he stubbornly refused to part with it, claiming that it would upset the estate's spirits. We always answered that his constant drinking of spirits upset us.

Upon arriving, I was quick to call appraisers to examine the antiques in the vault. After a few months, most of them were gone, netting roughly twenty thousand pounds. What remained, besides some dusty furniture that no one desired, was the diamond. I hadn't sold it yet on account of the locals, who had shown up to my attempted auction and driven the buyers away. However, I had met some of those interested, including a German doctor by the name of Hermann Schultz, a protestant theologian. How a doctor had acquired three hundred thousand pounds, I did not know, but another man's accounts is no business of my own. I also ignored what a doctor would want a 24-carat diamond for, but a buyer is a buyer. I quickly contacted him and, to the locals' great displeasure, I sold the diamond.

The estate had always had a sinister feel to it, which I attributed to its age, but it seemed to grow even more so after I sold the diamond. The shadows seemed to grow darker, and at night I could hear a faint howling, although there were no dogs on the grounds. The estate's staff, as well as the locals, started to leave one by one, none of them giving warning of their departure. I did not know what superstitions surrounded the diamond, and I was not interested. I was above the common beliefs, for I was an enlightened man, or at least I thought myself one. Soon, only the butler and I remained in the manor, and I preferred that. I now had the peace and solitude needed to study the stars, something that the castle was well placed to do, for I could even see the distant Nerla star, which was believed to have control over the living.

November that year was especially cold and the days were especially short, giving me plenty of time to study the stars. On the fourteenth, I had finally sold off the last antiques and went to sleep satisfied. It was a short and restless sleep, and several times I imagined seeing my butler and a hooded man standing over me, but it was of course just a dream.

The next day, I was out in the now deserted city square when I noticed a hooded man resembling the one in my dream, although he was not in the presence of my butler. I quickly hurried home, although I did not make much of it for this was not the first time I imagined being followed.

I dreamed of him again the next night. This time, I saw the hooded figure in my room, but from him was emanating a strange glow that seemed to produce a warm sensation throughout my entire body. The rest of the dream was a blur, but I remember him slowly talking to me to the sound of drums – before he plunged my head underwater.

It was months before I saw the hooded figure again, in both my dreams and the real world, although I now realize that there is only a very thin line separating them. I was sleeping with my good friend Will, when I woke up to hear a slight buzzing sound. The night was still young and it was pitch black outside, except for what appeared to be a ray of starlight that landed squarely on my friend's face. Then suddenly, as if possessed, he stood up and left the house, only to return hours later, smelling of sewer waste and wearing a dark hood.

I do not know if he was really the man I saw in my dreams, and I am even unsure as to whether he really had left the house that night. It is quite possible that my then deep-seated paranoia had made me delirious. However, upon seeing him return that way, I felt this great sense of foreboding as my heart began to beat rapidly, my temples felt warm as if licked by the flames of hell. I

did not stay to find out more. I left my castle, not wanting to sell it as I wanted to have nothing more to do with the wretched place. I talked to various astrophysicists and priests about the matter, and all agreed that I was delirious, maybe even psychotic, although that is simply because they have not seen what my eyes have. I willingly turned myself into an asylum, where they confiscated all of my belongings
– an empty diary that has never been opened, and glasses engravedwith my name: "Hermann Shultz".

End of corresponce.

Case #13029
Joad Nacer

Details not released
at this time.

CLAYTON HILL SANITARIUM

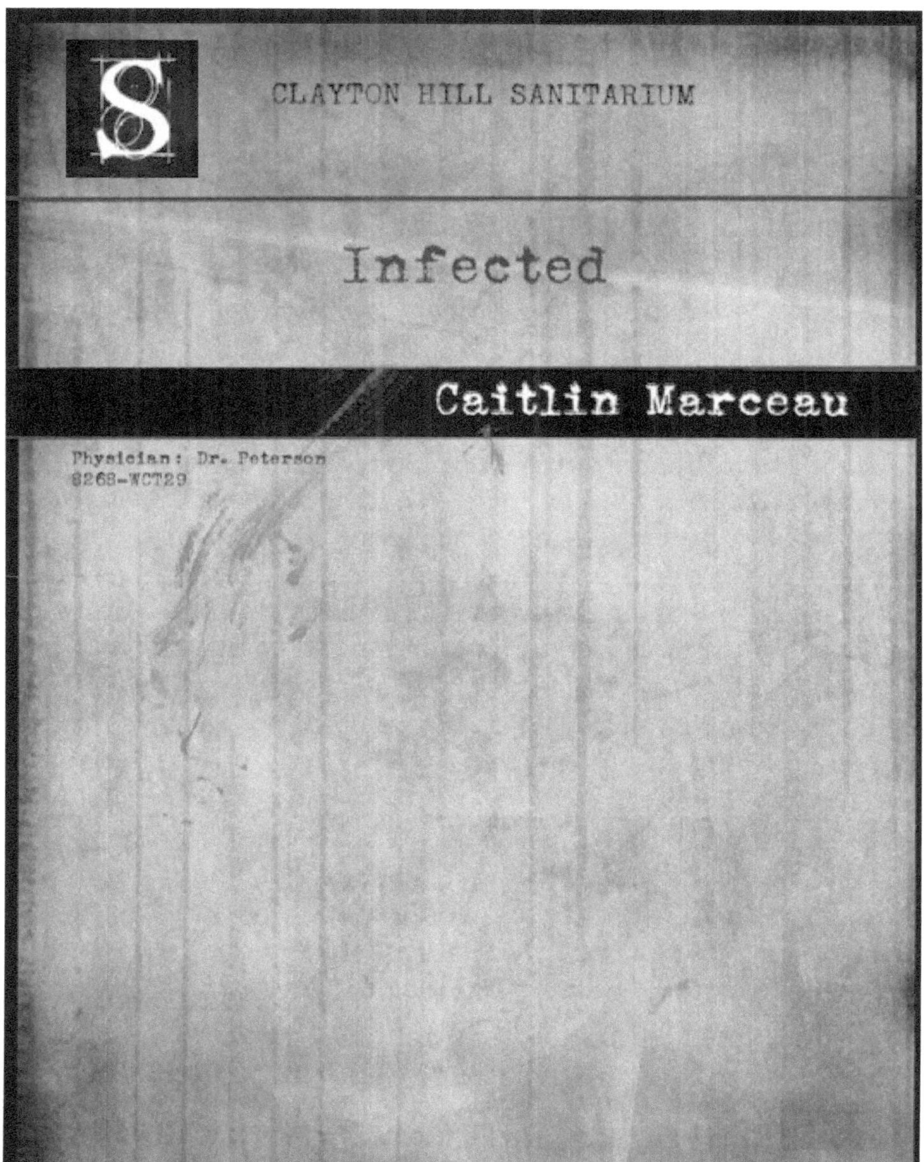

CLAYTON HILL SANITARIUM
Infected
Caitlin Marceau
Physician: Dr. Peterson
8268-WCT29

WE COLLECTIVELY SHUFFLE TOWARDS WHAT THEY'VE named "the mess hall." The chain link fence clinks in the wind, our stomachs growl loud. At first, I think I'm the only one who hears it, the gurgling and churning of acid and digestive fluids in an empty stomach, but the guards tighten their grips on their guns and put another foot between themselves and the fence. It's cold out, but the air feels good on my skin, cooling the sweat beading on my forehead.

The building in front of us is broken and run down. In its day it would have been beautiful; a tower made of polished glass, jutting out of the city skyline like a monument to human innovation. Now it stands before us cracked and covered in dirt. The front door has been removed from its hinges, leaving the building open and uninviting. We walk in, some slow, some eager, all ravenous. The scent of meat is strong enough to fill the yard and it draws us in. My heart hammers, nostrils flare, and I swallow the saliva pooling in my mouth.

I pass through the entrance, eyeing one of the empty places at a picnic table deep within. The room, what would have once been the lobby, looks as run down as the exterior. Most of the walls are covered in what could pass for Jackson Pollock paintings made of old blood and mud. The original gold paint, what little of it is still showing, is dull. Holes, some with the bullets still lodged inside, hide amongst the stains. The marble floor is cracked and chipped, marked by conflicts past. Where a receptionist once sat is a cage, not to keep things in but to keep us out. The guard inside doesn't look convinced the cage can hold much back, as he taps on the chain fencing with the butt of his gun when we get too close.

I sit down, the old wood of the bench creaking under my weight. The paper plate in front of me holds a slab of meat grilled enough to feel warm but not enough to be considered rare. I pick it up, licking my dry lips, looking at the people gathered in the centre of the room. They stare at the rest of us, mortified. They're new to the pens and still hold on to hope that this is just a bad dream. I pick up the beef with my bare hands. They continue to watch, wide eyed, and I try to ignore them as I lift the slab of meat to my mouth.

One of them locks eyes with me and I stare into them.

Then I rip into the flesh, pulling it apart and crushing it between my teeth.

***

Thin beams of light shine out from between the cracks in the blinds, turning the tips of Philibert's straw blonde hair golden and making me smile. There hasn't been sun like this, real sun, in ages. There's only been the fluorescent glow of the day lamps, which hardly illuminate the smoky city, for a very long time. It makes me happy, warming me from the pit of my stomach to the tips of my fingers.

Today feels like a good day.

I stretch out in the hard bed, waking tired limbs and finding comfort in the rough sheets that scratch my skin. It's almost time to get up, I know the morning siren's going to ring any minute now, but I don't want to leave this spot. I want to spend the day looking at the sunshine from the warmth of my bed. I want to pull off the blinds and soak it all up, absorb as much as I can before it's gone again.

I push myself closer to Philibert, enjoying the warmth his body radiates in the cold room. He's hogged most of the blankets, again, and has rolled halfway onto my side of the mattress. He snores lightly, enough to keep me up when I'm trying to fall asleep but not loud enough to wake me once I'm under, and nestles into his pillow. I curl up beside him, pulling on the sheets to better cover myself against the fall cold. He opens his eyes and frowns, rolling himself over to his side of the bed again.

"Your skin's ice cold, woman," he says sleepily, "don't rub up against me with it." He pushes some of the blankets towards me, warm from his body heat, and I burry myself in them.

He sighs as I cuddle up to his back, tossing an arm over his side and touching his chest lazily. My hand trails slowly down, playing with the waist of his boxers, and I notice the tips of his mouth pull up in a tired smile. He sighs even louder, as the siren to wake the city wails, and interrupts the moment. He grumbles to himself as he gets out of bed, kicking the blankets off and heading to the washroom. I watch him walk, enjoying the way his muscles move under the skin of his lean frame. He crosses the small room, walking quickly on the cold scratched floor and closes the bathroom door behind him. There's the squeaking of taps then the familiar sound of water beating against the ceramic of the tub.

"Hey!" I call to him through the door, "it's supposed to be my turn for a shower. You had one yesterday."

He doesn't answer me and I realize he probably can't hear me under all the water. I hop out of the bed, crossing the room in a few quick strides and open the washroom door a crack.

"Philibert, it's my turn for a shower today. What are you doing?" "I need one."

"You had your turn yesterday..."

He doesn't say anything, just continues to soap up behind the shower doors.

"Philibert..."

"Can't you just take yours tomorrow, Tiph? I have to go to work, and I'm all sweaty from helping to rebuild the school in the East district yesterday. You have the day off, so take yours tomorrow. Ok?"

He sounds frustrated, and he does have a point. It's not like I have anywhere important to be today.

"Sure, yeah, no problem."

I close the door behind me and head further down the hall to the kitchen. The walls on the way are empty, no photos hung in glass frames. Holes and scratches from nails poorly hammered adorn them instead, the memories safe in our heads and the paper saved for something more useful. Only a finger painting, Philibert's name and mine in a lopsided heart, hints to some kind of life inside this unit. I walk into the kitchen, stomach growling, and search for something to eat.

The floor is covered in all different tiles, a mosaic of anything that would fit and stick to the ground. The counters are old and stained by older food that wasn't able to be fully washed off. The doors are off two of the cupboards, and the wooden door of the pantry doesn't match. I like how it looks, a patchwork kitchen, and how it reminds me of the quilts my mother used to make for me growing up. Bits and pieces of everything around me, all stuck together to make something new.

I pull a box of cereal from the shelf then measure a perfect cup, dumping it into a chipped orange bowl. The cereal is brown and looks like something I may have fed my guinea pig when it was still alive. I then pour a measured cup of powdered milk into the bowl, mix it with a metal spoon, and dig in. Despite the bitter taste it leaves in my mouth, it fills my stomach and meets the minimum requirements for nutritional value.

Once I'm done, I put the bowl in the sink next to the dirty dishes from supper last night, and head back to the bedroom to get changed. Philibert's nearly done dressing, the brown pants and navy top fresh from the laundry complex. The shirt is too loose on him and the pants are too tight, but there's nothing he can do but hope that the next batch of uniforms they send fit better. They wash all the soiled uniforms together, and deliver clean ones once a week. All the sizes are standardized, and even though he's a medium, the uniforms never fit him like they should.

"What are your plans for lunch?" I ask, pulling my civilian clothes out from the bottom drawer of the dresser.

"The same as always. Why?"

"Well I was thinking, maybe we could go over to Sarah's for lunch? We haven't seen her in a while, and I know she has the day off... plus her kids will be at school."

He pulls the shirt tight, making sure it's neatly tucked into his pants, then runs his fingers over the collar to check it's properly folded.

"I mean, if you have too much work to do, that's fine. I'll go alone or maybe we can see her tonight..."

"No, no, that should be fine," he says quickly, picking his cardkey off the nightstand and slipping into his breast pocket. The second siren wails, telling the city the work day is about to being. He crosses the room and kisses me quickly on the lips before rushing off down the hall. Fabric rustles followed by a zipper sliding closed.

"Love you!" I call after him, hoping he heard me over the loud slam of the door.

I head to the washroom and run a cloth under the warm water, careful to use only what I need. Once the hot water tank is empty, it stays empty until the end of the week. I still need a shower tomorrow and dishes still need to get done. I wash myself down and rinse the rag out, leaving it to dry on the edge of the sink. I quickly brush my teeth and try to comb out my long brown waves, eager to spend as much time in the sun as I can before the night comes. The plastic teeth pull painfully at the knots in my hair, making me grimace. I put the comb on the bathroom shelf, tie my locks back in a ponytail, and hurriedly pull my clothes on. The grey pants and t-shirt wash out my already pale skin, but at least they fit me properly. I sit on the edge of the bed and pull on my socks. A beam of light falls across my face, making me smile.

***

I wipe my mouth with the back of my hand. The cow's blood stains my skin red but camouflages into my crimson jumper. My stomach is full, but I'm still hungry. I eye the paper plate of the man sitting next to me and clench my jaw. I look away, staring at the ceiling, and run my hand through my hair absentmindedly. Long brown strands come out, sticking to my dirty fingers and my breath catches in my throat. I rub my palm against my thigh, some of my brown hair sticking to my uniform and the rest falling onto the ground. My hands begin to quiver, so I interlace my fingers and place them in my lap, trying to think about anything other than the slab of half-eaten meat next to me or how my body is beginning to shut down.

I must look like Martha did when I saw her last; her curly black hair falling out like a cancer patient in chemo, dark circles under her eyes, jaundice creeping into her olive skin. It was only a few days ago they moved her to Pen B. I wonder if she ever saw her boyfriend again or if he recognized her through his fever. I wonder if Philibert will know me when he sees me again, if he'll cry at my patchy scalp and blueing nails. I look at the plastic wedding ring he gave me and I hope they let him have it back after I'm dead; I don't want them to burn it like they do everything else.

"Get off!" someone screams.

It's the girl who watched me eat, the girl who couldn't look away. She can't be older than twelve, maybe thirteen. Her scraggly hair is in two braids and, unlike the rest of us, she looks good in red. Her skin hasn't yellowed enough to look harsh in the clothes they've given us, and if it wasn't for the fevered look in those brown eyes I'd have thought she was healthy.

A man is hanging on to her arm, saliva dripping from his open mouth on to the marble floor. He pulls her close, the only evidence of the meal that was on his plate a red stain on the white paper. She

86

pulls away from him hard, straining against him, her shoulder being wrenched nearly out of its socket as she tries to get away. We all watch, but none of us move to help her. I don't know if it's from apathy or shock, but not one of us come to her aid as the man throws himself at her, teeth digging into her upper arm.

The guards begin to shout instructions to us and at each other. The one in the cage radios to his colleagues that there's a "situation" in the mess hall. They begin ushering us out of the room, forcing us back the way we came. Everyone around me gets up and begins shambling towards the door. One of the guards fires his gun into the ceiling, spraying us with dust and plaster, bellowing for us to get a move on.

I stay seated and watch the girl, the human in me unable to look away and the monster I'm becoming not wanting to. She's screaming for me to do something, looking at me with pleading wild eyes. She kicks out, flailing, as the man takes another bite of her arm. He tries to better position himself on top of her, the rubber of his shoe slipping on the wet floor. He pins her down and rips into her throat, pulling away with a mouthful of skin and stringy muscle. She slowly stops fighting, her head turned towards me as she dies.

The room is nearly empty of people when I finally get up and begin to make my way to the doors. More guards enter the room from a staircase in the back, one of them carrying two large black bags. I turn away from them and begin pushing past the last few people, trying to get out of the hall faster now. Their boots thud heavily against the floor, and it reminds me of the beating of a war drum.

Then they stop as suddenly as they started. Two shots are fired fast, then after a moment a third rings out. I stop moving and look over my shoulder. The man is unrecognizable, dead atop the little girl. Even though her head is turned away, gazed fixed on where I sat, I can feel her eyes watching me.

As I move into the yard, I realize the answer to my question is no. How can I expect Philibert to recognize me, when even I don't?

***

87

The city used to be so beautiful in the fall. The leaves on the trees turning orange and red, squirrels running over lawns in search of food for the winter, the air cool enough for a coat but warm enough for a walk.

Now everything's cold and grey. Grey and brown really; dry grass, earth and ash. Gardens are empty and starved of water. Dirt and dust coats the buildings, so heavily in places that it's hard to remember them without tinted windows. I walk carefully, planning out each step before I take it. There isn't much in the way of rubble to trip on, most of it having been collected and taken away to the waste pile. They try to reuse or recycle as much as they can from the demolished homes, but whatever can't be given new life sits in the massive garbage heap. The small stones and cracks are what threaten to twist my ankles as I walk. But those always used to trip me up, when I'd wear stilettos and pants a size too tight.

I smile, enjoying the memories of high heels and days gone by.

I roll the sleeves of my jacket up, wanting to keep from the cold but also wanting to feel sun on my skin for the first time in weeks. When the bombs went off during the panic, we couldn't see the sun in the sky for months. Then, slowly, we began to see the shape of the sun from behind the clouds of smoke and dust. Now it's starting to peek out from behind the smog, but we all know it's going to be a long time before the air is clear enough for it to light up the city like it once did. Until then, we'll live behind the daytime fluorescents that flicker and buzz like fireflies.

I walk through the city districts, careful to keep to the sidewalks as trucks full of guards and supplies speed by. Their wheels kick up dust and make my eyes sting. I weave my way through the maze of streets and city districts. A black truck, with a neon yellow biohazard sign, rushes by and I hold my breath. Inside of the truck it carries the diseased and the dying. It transports the last of the plague out of the city, keeping the rest of us safe from the infection that decimated the population over eight years ago. I watch it speed down the road, taking a sharp turn out of sight. I exhale loud and roll my shoulders, trying to work the sudden tension out of them before continuing my walk.

I turn off the main road that runs through the two largest districts. I begin to roam what would've once been a quiet niche of the city. The rich families used to live here. They'd spend money on overpriced homes designed to look like suburban townhouses, while having the luxuries only living in the heart of a metropolis could bring. It's eerily quiet, almost silent, like I'm the only one in the world left. As I walk further, the air gets thicker and full of ash. Then I hear a crackling on the wind and what sounds like screaming, and I follow it to its source.

One of the houses is being burned to the ground. A group of men stand in front of the home, donning protective gear and flamethrowers. Two fire trucks are parked close by, hoses ready and waiting should the fire get out of hand. I move closer, wanting to get a better view of the flames. The air is warm from the blaze and my hair sticks to the sweat on my skin. As I cross the strip of road to the yard, a gust of wind pushes a cloud of ash into me. The tiny particles force their way past my nostrils and into my lungs. I double over, coughing hard, my throat burning and eyes watering.

"Ma'am," someone calls.

I look up to see a member of the Patrol approaching. The gas mask he wears muffles his voice, and he moves towards me fast with his hand on the holster of his gun.

"Are you alright ma'am?" he asks slowly.

"Yes, yes," I sputter through coughs, "ash... breathe..."

The guard removes his hand from his gun and signals for two guards I hadn't noticed to stand down.

"Ma'am, I'm sorry, but you're not allowed to be this close. If you could just stand further back, please."

I nod and step away from him. I spit on the pavement next to me and cough again, this time to try and clear my throat.

"Why aren't you putting the fire out?" I ask, voice rough.

He looks back at the house, not meeting my gaze.

"We found... signs... of possible contamination with infections materials. As per standard protocol, we're eliminating all traces of the biohazard. Now, ma'am , if you'd kindly step ba-"

"I heard screaming," I cut him off.

He stands straighter, looking me in the eye this time, before answering.

"You must be mistaken. Now, ma'am, I won't ask you again to stand back."

I nod and move to the other side of the road, hand on my chest as I watch the fire burn.

***

I throw up in the corner of the yard, but no one cares. Not even the guards who will have to clean it. Stomach acid and everything I've eaten in the last day hits the ground, mixing with the dirt and grass. Some of it splashes onto my uniform and shoes. My stomach churns, hungry for the food I've just given up. I lean against the fence and bend over, letting my head hang. The liquefied contents of my stomach slowly fill the cracks and craters of the ground, pooling around the solid chunks.

None of the sick men and women roaming around the yard notice me. None of them seem upset by the incident in the mess hall, like they've seen this a hundred times before.

Maybe they have.

I slump to the ground, sweat beading down my face, and unzip the top of my crimson one-piece. The air on my chest feels good, but not enough to cool me down. I unzip the uniform even more, exposing me from the sides of my breasts to my navel. I want to rip the clothing off, to walk through the pen naked. Even though the fabric is thin, it feels as warm as a parka with the blazing fever. I lick my lips, realizing how dry they are and how dry my cracked, yellow, skin is.

The wind ruffles my hair. I take a fistful in my hand and pull slowly, testing its strength. My scalp releases the strands, giving up the brown locks Philibert used to play with. Not all of them come out, some of them clinging to my head. I pull harder, ripping them out. With both hands, I pull, tearing all I can out from the roots. It doesn't hurt like I know it should.

I slip my right arm out from my uniform, then my left. I let the top of the one-piece hang limp on the ground around me, and pull my legs up to my chest in an attempt to fake modesty and get comfortable. I lie back against the cold metal fence, close my eyes and try to sleep.

***

Approaching the door, I pull a cardkey from my back pocket, worried for just a second that it may have fallen out on the jog over, and hand it to the guard stationed out front. He frowns at me, and swipes the card with his handheld reader. It beeps twice, giving me clearance to the building's inner entrance.

The heavy steel doors open and I walk through. Another officer waits inside and a woman in scrubs sits behind a reception desk.

"Good afternoon," she says with a bored smile, "how may I help you today?"

"I'm here to see Philibert Cabral. He works upstairs in-
" "Data analysis," she finishes for me. I nod as she
continues on.

"I'm just going to need some information, if that's alright?" she asks, opening a binder lined with sign in sheets. She flips to an empty one and waits for me to answer.

I nod again, knowing to refuse is to be escorted out.

"Your name, please."

"Tiphany Cabral."

"Relation?"

"Wife."

"Date of your most recent
vaccination?" "September 17th, 2018.
So, yesterday."

"Wonderful. And, last one, do you have a checkpoint paper from today?"

"No, sorry."

She jots something down and opens one of the desk drawers, taking out a glass vial with a cotton swap sealed inside. She reaches into a box on her desk, pulling out a pair of plastic gloves and putting them on.

"No problem. I'm just going to need to take a cheek swab to make sure you're clean, and then you'll be issued a checkpoint paper that will give you clearance to public buildings for the next three hours. After that, you'll be required to submit to another swab."

"No problem."

The receptionist/nurse picks up the vial with the swab and she approaches me. She uncaps the tube and I open my mouth, noticing that the guard has moved closer to me. I wait for her to finish scratching me with the cotton tip, trying not to gag when she puts it in too far. She puts the swab back in the glass and walks back to her desk.

Behind it is a counter, government issued, cluttered with test-tube racks, labels, a few bottles of blue liquid and a disposal unit for hazardous materials. She slides the vial in a holder and pours some of the blue liquid into it, filling just enough to cover the cotton end of the swab. I cross my arms, always annoyed during this procedure; I've had my shots kept up to date and there's no reason for me to need testing. I know what the outcome's going to be, it's always-

"I'm sorry Mrs. Cabral, but your test results are showing up purple, indicating a trace of infection," she says slowly.

It takes me a moment to decipher her words and once I do, it takes me even longer to figure out how to react to them.

"Excuse me?"

"Your results have turned up positive for potential infection." "But it's blue."

"No, ma'am, that's purple," she insists, showing me the tube as proof.

"I don't mean that's blue. I mean my results are always blue. Always."

I can feel sweat on the back of my neck and my hands feel unsteady.

The room tilts a bit to the left and I wonder if I should brace myself against a wall to keep from falling. It's a mistake. It has to be. She probably poured the wrong liquid in. All the blue solutions are unmarked, so how's she supposed to tell the right one apart from the rest?

"Yes, but because of th-"

"I'm not infected. I'm clearly not rabid," I tell her matter-of-factly. I can hear the guard muttering under his breath and from the corner of my eye I realize he's holding a walkie. His free hand is resting on the stun-gun in his holster, his eyes fixed on me.

"Please, ma'am, if you'd just relax a moment and take a deep breath. These in-house results are never conclusive. They only show that you have bacteria in your blood similar to that of the disease which, in your case, could be the result of a fresh inoculation," she tells me in a soothing voice.

"So then what's the problem? If you know it's from my shot just let me in," I try and reason, drumming my fingers restlessly against my thigh.

"As I'm sure you're aware, standard procedure is that we isolate the source of potential infection, have a full medical exam administered, and upon a clean bill of health you'll be released."

"Released? So I'm a prisoner now?" I ask, throat much too tight. "A patient if you're sick and an inconvenienced citizen if you're not. It's just a precaution to ensure public safety, ma'am. If you'd just follow Clay, he'll escort you to a waiting area until the proper transport arrives."

"Alone? What about Philibert? He's going to wonder where I am. He'll be worried. He'll want to know what's being done."

"We'll inform him immediately and he'll be brought down to the holding bay to accompany you to the appropriate facility. If you'd just please follow Clay..."

The guard comes up beside me, his hand now resting directly on the stun gun, and leads me to a side door I hadn't noticed before. Of course there'd be a side door; if I was rabid, they wouldn't want me back on the streets to become a roamer, but they wouldn't want me in the building either. He slides a cardkey in the reader and it gives a shrill beep before the lock releases. He pushes the thick steel door open to reveal a sitting room that could've come from an old IKEA catalogue.

Crisp white walls, squishy sofas, and some chairs that look morelike art than they do comfortable, all circle a long white coffee table stacked with books. The door clangs shut behind me, and I spin on my heel. The guard has sealed me in, alone, and I take a seat on one of the couches. From this angle, a thin gap between the curtains is visible and I notice a strip of silver.

Another door.

My heart's pounding so hard that I think my ribs are rattling. I fold my arms across my chest and cross my left leg over my right. I can't have the infection. I can't because I just took my shots. The vaccine keeps the virus away, keeps us from going rabid, from turning cannibal, from the devastation the world survived.

But what if I'm sick?

But I'm not.

Why is this room so warm?

I wait for what feels like years until I hear the now familiar sound of a lock unlocking. I look over my shoulder at the door and see my husband, escorted by the less than pleasant guard.

"Philibert!" I say his name like it's the most beautiful word I've ever said. I stand up quickly and turn towards him.

He takes a step away from me, like something's pushed him back. His gaze darts around the room quickly, constantly shifting from me to his surroundings. The guard raises his hand, palm towards me and hand open.

"Ma'am, I'm going to have to ask you to stay back."

"Seriously?"

"Protocol."

I stare at the guard, my eyes stinging and I try not to look as upset as I feel. None of us speak for a moment. The Philibert gives me a big smile, his lips stretched too tight and too wide, trying to diffuse the tension.

"Hey, Tiph," he says much too gently, "how're you feeling?"

"Fine. I'm feeling perfectly fine and this is all bullshit. You have to
know that. Please tell me you know that."

"Of course, babe. Of course it is and we're going to get all of this straightened out, I promise."

I raise my eyebrow and shake my head, looking anywhere but at him.

"You've never, in your life, called me 'babe' so don't start now.
Don't try to fucking pacify me with a pet name, ok?" I say loudly.

The guard moves forward, ready to jump between us should I
suddenly spring forward and attack.

"I'm sorry," I say taking a step back, "I'm just really stressed, ok?"
"Yeah, Tiph, I know. But you're going to be fine. The transport is going to be here soon, they'll run a few tests, ask you a few questions and I'll meet you there in a couple hours," he tells me, stepping out
from behind the guard.

"Meet me there? Aren't you coming with me?"

Philibert clears his throat and straightens his shirt before answering.
His face seems flushed and he won't meet my gaze.

"They need me to answer a few questions about you, to help them retrace your steps. What you do, who you've been with the last 24 hours, that kind of stuff. The second they're done, I'll head right over."

"Why would they ask you where I've been? You've been here all day, it's not like you're going to know. And who I've been with?

Sexually? Just you and you know that." He shifts his weight from foot to foot.

"Tiph, I know, but that's what they want so I'm going to be as helpful as I can. Anything to help you get better is my priori-"

"I'm not sick!"

The guard points the stun gun directly at my chest.

"I know. I know you're not, Tiph. We'll get this all sorted and you'll be out in no time. Promise."

Philibert walks away from me and heads to the door. The guard backs up, not turning his back to me and swipes his cardkey in the reader. The door opens with another beep.

"I'll see you in a bit, Tiph," Philibert says as he steps through to the other side.

The guard follows him through, gun still raised, and shuts the door behind them.

***

I wake up in a room as naked as I feel. No single piece of furniture adorns the small quarters. The light fixtures are flat and too high for me to reach, and there's no doorknob where the door is. Three of the walls are white and, like everything else in these pens, show signs of a struggle. Old stains peak out from under hasty paint jobs. Scratches cover the floor and dig deep into the plaster on the walls. The fourth wall is made of glass, and I see another room like this one on the other side.

I'm curled in the fetal position, my crimson jumper replaced by a white hospital gown, my wedding band still on my finger. For the first time since being infected, I don't feel warm. My skin isn't hot or too tight on my body. I feel healthy again. I feel better. I push myself into a sitting position and smile as the wood underneath me feels cold. Cold. I run my hands over my scalp and the skin is smooth and soft. I inspect my arms, my legs and I even pull my gown up to run my hands over my chest. The scars and marks that littered my body are gone.

I feel like me again.

In the other room the door opens and Philibert walks in.

***

"Mrs. Cabral?" a man asks from the door behind the drapes, pushing them aside with his clipboard.

"Yes," I seethe from my spot on the sofa.

As though there's anyone else in here.

"If you'd kindly bring all your personal belongings and follow me." He leads me through a narrow tunnel to an alleyway. A black truck bearing the yellow biohazard sign is parked and waiting. I stop dead in my tracks, not wanting to get a step closer to the vehicle. The guard looks at me and waits patiently for me continue onwards. I swallow hard and keep moving. It's just a mix up and I need to be brave. No, not brave; complacent. I've had my vaccination and there's no need

to be brave when I'm immune.

Inside are seats fastened to the walls with harnesses to keep people secured. Two of the seats are already occupied. One of them is a woman, late fifties, who looks as frightened as I feel. She looks at me and recoils, shrinking back in her chair. The other one, a boy in his late teens, doesn't seem to understand what's happening, and his eyes look wide and unfocussed. His skin's pale, yellowing in patches, and I know he'll be rabid soon.

He looks like every poster for the disease that I'd ever seen; warning us to report any and all roamers, listing the signs of infection beside the photo of someone who used to be human. Fever, bloodshot eyes, yellowing skin, incoherent speech, sexual aggression, violent outbursts, rage and hunger. Philibert used to say the rabid want only the three animal Fs; to feed, fuck, and fight. The man mutters something, trying to lean forward. He's watching me now, and his eyes are void of intelligent thought.

"I'm not getting in this thing with him in here," I tell the officer, eyes fixed on the boy.

"Ma'am, the harnesses will keep him restrained, and I'll put you next to the woman on the opposite wall. I promise you, we take security measures to prevent patients from getting free. Now, if you'll just take a seat," he tells me, pointing to a chair near the old woman.

I climb the steps of the truck and sit. The officer ties me in and I feel like a prisoner. Each hand is fastened to the opposite shoulder, my legs are strapped to the floor of the truck, and my body is secured in a harness that looks more like a straight jacket than anything close to seatbelt. The journey to the medical centre is a long one. It's at least an hour's drive away and isolated from the city.

Along the way, we pick up more people. Two middle aged men, both yellow around the edges, and a woman who can't be much older than I am. She's harnessed in next to me. She doesn't seem sick, but doesn't seem worried either.

"I'd shake your hand if I had one free," she jokes.

I can't help but chuckle, even if it feels a bit strange for me to be laughing at a time like this.

"Martha," she says, winking.

"Tiphany Cabral."

She gives me a once over, frowning. "You look too young to be a wife." "What?"

She nods to my left hand, where a plastic ring from a costume shop rests around my finger.

"Either you put that on the wrong hand this morning, or your husband made do with what he had."

I close my eyes and smile, nodding to her. "You know how it was; people thought the end was nigh and figured it was their last chance to get hitched. Suddenly standards didn't matter and people took what they could get," I explain.

"You seem happy about settling, though."

"I am. Well, I didn't really settle, but I probably wouldn't have gotten married to him at 16 either," I admit.

Martha nods, understanding. She looks around the truck and hums to herself. She's comfortable here, at ease, and her courage makes me strong.

***

Philibert walks close to the glass partition, watching me. He hasn't shaven in a while, the stubble on his chin longer than it was when we last spoke. He's in his grey civilian uniform, but the shirt looks wrinkled and dirty. He puts a hand against the glass and smiles at me, eyes dull.

I put my hand on the glass and smile back, leaning my head on the window.

97

He pulls away for a moment, before putting his hand back and leaning in close.

"Why do you look so upset? I mean, I know you weren't expecting me to be bald, I wasn't expecting me to go bald, but I'm better."

My voice catches in my throat and I feel my eyes sting as the words hang in the air.

"I'm better," I whisper this time.

***

I try and relax into my chair, but the straps pull uncomfortably on my chest. I wiggle in them, huffing and puffing. With all the people, and the harness around me, it's hot in the truck.

"Ugh, these straps are biting into my skin; I think they're cutting off my circulation. Hey," I shout in hopes someone will hear me, "can you loosen these, please? It's too tight."

No one from the front cabin of the truck answers so I call even louder.

Nothing.

"I think they're used to hearing people yell. It's probably why they aren't answering," Martha tells me.

I frown, but know she's right.

"So, how'd you end up here? Get bitten by a roamer?" she asks casually, like two friends talking over a drink at a bar.

"Oh, I'm not sick," I tell her quickly, "this is just a mistake." "Of course."

"No, really. I had my shot yesterday, so my test showed signs of possible infection. I'm not actually rabid," I laugh. "And you? Did they screw up your vaccine too?"

"Oh, no. I'm definitely infected."

"What?" I ask, unsure I heard her properly.

"I'm infected."

"How? I mean, you can't be sure. Everyone's been given shots, the antivirus. I mean, it could just be a mist-"

"My boyfriend came home from the plant last night. A roamer had attacked him and bit one of his fingers off. The vaccines can only do so much, you know? So, we knew he was done for. A dead man walking kind of thing," she tells me in a matter of fact tone.

"Anyways, we wait the night, hoping that maybe he'll be able to

98

fight off the infection. He wasn't. He started turning around breakfast. I don't want to be here without him, and I don't want him dying alone and afraid. So, I slept with him for the last time."

"You what?" I ask horrified.

"Slept with him," she says calmly. "They came and got him early this afternoon, while I was out. When I got home and he wasn't there, I called them to come collect me."

"You're insane!"

"No, no. It's brilliant. This way we'll be in the pens together. We'll both turn and won't be alone."

"You're fucking crazy," I hiss, pulling as far away from her as I can.

I'd heard rumours of suicide by roamer, but never believed them. Who would choose this for themselves? What was she thinking? The teen across from us begins wailing, beating the back of his head against the truck wall.

"Crazy? Crazy would have been to go on without him, to keep on fighting. Giving in is the sanest thing we can do."

***

He looks like he hasn't slept in a very long time. There's a knocking, and then the door to Philibert's room opens a crack.

"Sir, my name is Dr. Stephenson. I've been charting your wife's condition since her admission to the facility. May I come in? It's important I speak with you."

Philibert nods. The door opens to grant access to a man in a white lab coat. Under it he wears the regulated purple uniform of a healthcare worker and carries a clear plastic clipboard. He watches me, expression blank, and flips to a page in his notes. I pull myself off the window and smile to the doctor.

"It's nice to finally meet you. They told me a physician was assigned to me, but they never said who."

"How did she contract it?" Philibert asks bluntly.

The doctor looks back down at his paper, jots something down, and turns his attention to Philibert.

"She told the admissions nurse she'd accidentally inhaled fresh ash at the scene of a decontamination fire. She hadn't been wearing a protective mask and likely ingested biohazardous material." After

99

a moment of silence passes between them, the doctor continues. "We need to discuss her options."

Philibert doesn't bother looking up, but rather he continues to stare at me. He furrows his brow and exhales deeply, his warm breath leaving a mark on the glass.

"What options?" I ask, my attention now on the doctor.

"I know it's difficult to talk about, Mr. Cabral, but it's important that we know what to do during this final stage."

"What final stage?" I ask.

When both are silent, I knock on the glass. Both of them take a step back from the window and Philibert looks unsettled.

"As you've been explained, those infected have a terminal prognosis. Tiphany is degenerating steadily, and if she continues at this rate she'll, regrettably, pass on within the week."

"What the hell do you mean by 'pass on'? I'm fine!" I shout, banging my open hand against the window.

"Right now, her brain is shutting down. She's lost the proper function of her kidneys and liver; her respiratory rate is much too high and her pulse much too low. She's losing circulation in her extremities, as you can see by her blue fingers and toes," the doctor lies.

I look at my body, my skin pink and healthy, my fingers intact and nails well groomed.

Why is he lying to Philibert?

I'm healthy, I'm cured, and I just want to go home.

"From what we're able to tell," he continues, "she's also lost the ability to reason. Two guards found her huddled in the yard, naked, and ripping out her hair. Lu-"

"Liar! It fell out! My hair, it fell out! Stop it!" I shout, slapping my hands against the glass, "Phil, can't you see he's lying?"

Why can't they hear me?

"-ckily they were able to tranquilize her and bring her here without the use of excessive force. We had to shave her head for her own protection and we've done the best we can with her self-inflicted wounds. As you can see, she's unable to communicate using language and we don't believe she's able to understand it either."

Philibert turns away from me.

"What can you do?"

"We can either keep her isolated like she is and let the infection take its course or..."

"Or?" Philibert and I ask in unison.

"Or there's always euthanasia."

Philibert's shoulders tense and he folds his arms over his chest.

"The hell there is," I yell.

"I know it isn't what you want to hear," the doctor says in a soothing tone, "but there's nothing else we can do for her. It's the humane option for those in her state. It's quick, painless, and allows those infected to keep their integrity."

The hair stand up on the back of my neck.

"If you need some time to think about it, I can always come back later... I understand this isn't an easy decision."

The doctor clicks his pen, retracting the ballpoint back into the plastic shaft and slipping it into his breast pocket. He pulls a walkie from his lab coat with his free hand and presses down on a button, bringing it close to his mouth to speak.

"No, wait," Philibert cuts in. His voice is thick and he looks back at me, not bothering to fake a smile. "I... I don't want her to suffer like this. You're sure she won't feel anything?" he asks.

"No! No!" I yell, beating my fists against the glass, willing the window to break.

This can't be happening. I'm fine, I'm fine!

"Just the prick of a needle, like a booster shot or a vaccine."

***

The truck begins to bounce up and down as we drive over what can only be a gravel driveway. I shout for them to get me out of here, that there's a mistake. Don't they know there's a mistake? I'm not like the others, I'm not sick. I'm not insane. I'm not rabid. Can't they see that?

"If you're husband was sick," she says over the boy's screaming, "if your husband was dying, what would you have done?"

There's a sickening crunch and a gurgling sound that follows. The teen has cracked his head open against the wall, blood dripping onto the floor below him. Yet still, he thwacks his head against the truck, beating his brains in, shouting, until he's finally quiet.

The truck comes to a halt. The back doors squeal in protest as the guards open them. Sounds of men talking, people screaming, a gun firing all rush in and greet us.

We're finally at the pens.

***

I wake up to bright lights and the smell of disinfectant. My eyes sting and my throat feels like it's been rubbed down with sandpaper. My head hurts and the room is spinning. They've wheeled a gurney into the white room and tied me to it. I turn my head towards the glass wall and see Philibert watching me. There are crow's feet where smooth skin used to be. His straw-coloured hair looks like dry grass and his bright eyes are dark.

Two men enter my room. One's carrying a sheet and the other, the doctor, a syringe.

"How'd this one contract it?" the orderly asks.

"She was recently vaccinated with batch 19," the doctor explains as he pricks my skin with the tip of the needle and shoots fire up my arm.

In the other room, a man walks in and gives Philibert a small brown envelope. He turns the package open and my wedding band slides into his open hand. He looks at me one last time before turning away, not wanting to watch me die. He walks to the door and pushes it open.

"If they're not careful," the orderly mumbles, "they're going to have another outbreak on their hands."

I feel tired, groggy. It's getting harder to hear them and the lights seem brighter, making my eyes hurt.

"I know. She's the seventh subject that's been brought in post-inoculation. But at least we know this test batch was a failure."

I watch the door shut behind Philibert and I close my eyes.

The End.

Case #48764

Caitlin Marceau

Caitlin Marceau is an author and professional editor living and working in Montreal. She prefers to focus her time on works of horror and journalism, but has also been published for poetry as well as experimental fiction. She is currently a student at Concordia University with a Major in creative writing. For more of her writing check out IXDaily.com, Shalomlife.com and SoundonSight.org.

CLAYTON HILL SANITARIUM
Fragments
Emir Skalonja
Physician: Dr. Peterson
S268-WCT29

To sam, Jackie was his whole world. He clung onto her as if she were his last breath of air keeping him suffocating.

She was the friendly shadow over his eyes keeping the ugliness of the world from getting in. Above all, she built a fence around his heart and made herself a willing prisoner of it, keeping the love for the two of them.

There was little in the way of them being together, very little in the way of their love and happiness that many of who knew them best, were rather jealous of it.

Sam met Jackie in the senior year of high school and since the day they met, they had been inseparable. They went through their ups and downs; hand in hand they stood against the world and whatever it decided to throw against them. Many said it was just kid's love, they were young and it will all fade away the same way it had come into their lives. Parent's from both sides claimed that the two should focus on their studies, focus on the careers ahead of them, put the love in the back seat of the car that was moving way too fast on the congested highway where accidents were bound to happen and those innocent and pure bound to get hurt. Those voices only became a murmur that would eventually fade away until it was just the two of them.

"I'd live in a box if it meant I'd live there with you," Jackie always said and right after she'd say it, she'd kiss Sam on the tip of his nose. He'd smile back and say, "Right back at ya."

College years came and went and the two were married. They bought a house. Each started their own careers, Sam a semi successful writing career that had its shares of ups and downs. Jackie became a mortgage specialist at a local bank. "At least one of them took the full responsibility for their lives and well being," friends would say and scoff. Jackie didn't care. She supported Sam every step of the way, reading and critiquing his writing.

Troubles started when Jackie was unable to conceive. They tried time and time again but nothing seemed to be working. Every resource, every hospital, every doctor was exhausted, visited and seen. There was not complex explanation to the issue other than Jackie was infertile. Neither wanted artificial insemination. "It's not ours. Ten years later someone shows up and wants to see what their sperm brought into this world," Sam said.

"There are disclosures, waivers," Jackie retorted."Those burn up and get forgotten very easily."

The two became distant. The distance between the them in bed became greater over the ensuing weeks, the middle getting colder and colder. A no man's land. Neither of them thought that something like not being able to have a child would drive them so far apart until they were merely strangers to each other. They went through the motions, acknowledging each other throughout the day, sharing a forced smile now and then. There was no more small talk, asking about the day and what the plans for the evening were. Those were long gone, replaced by exasperated sighs of frustration, grunts, one word answers and sometime even complete and utter silence.

Jackie became a recluse, while Sam's rather calm demeanor was replaced by violent mood swings and sudden loss of memory. He became increasingly interested in conspiracies which became a recurring theme of his upcoming stories.

It was after Christmas one year that Jackie came out and brought an envelope to Sam. Setting down the glass filled with Scotch, he opened the envelope and read the contents of the divorce papers.

Two days later, Jackie disappeared.

Sam looked for her, even going as far as filing a missing person's report. Weeks later, he came to terms that he would never again see Jackie.

***

Several months later Sam had the first of his disturbing dreams. These dreams were so vivid that when he woke up in cold sweat, he could not distinguish them from reality.

In the dream, he found himself in an abandoned town, covered in dust, as if it were a miniature in a globe that had dried out and been put on a shelf, forever forgotten.

In the dream, something beckoned him to move onward, to move toward the house that lay on the top of the hill at the end of the road. Though it had looked more like a church than a house. When he tried to move, his legs wouldn't obey, keeping him still in the spot at the very beginning of the street. The voice that commanded him from the house became increasingly louder until the noise was so disturbing his ear drums burst open in blood that trickled down his neck and onto his shaking shoulders. Then there was silence. This is when he would wake up.

The first time he had the dream, he dismissed it for just another nightmare.

The the second dream happened. And the third, until every dream he had each and every night was that one of him in the abandoned town, the voice calling to him.

Days passed and Sam became afraid of going to sleep. He saw his bed as his worst enemy, a death trap waiting for him to lay down and swallow him hole.

Then the dreams became his reality.

***

He stood at the beginning of the road he had always found himself on. There was a sign that was supposed to have the town's name written on it but the letters had been scratched off.

Beyond his gaze stretched a town, small and quiet, as if life had never been present here, though some small signs of existence gave themselves away. Dilapidated house were neatly lined up in single row on either side of the street and every three or four houses or buildings there was a small specialty shop: a candy store, a tailor, a post office, a mechanic and so on.

This time, though, there was no voice that came from the church on the hill. There was only silence.

Sam took a single step and found that his movements were not restricted in any way. He took another until it became a stroll down a deserted street. But somehow the town didn't feel deserted. It looked deserted but it definitely didn't feel deserted. As he walked down the street, he saw that all the windows on every house were either boarded up or covered with thick, dark curtains. Behind these simple obstacles, he could feel curious eyes that watched him move. Did all those eyes that watched him belong to the people who lived in this small town or to something else entirely? Just the thought of it made his body break out in gooseflesh. He couldn't see them but he could feel the eyes studying him, observing his every move, could feel them crawling all over his body. He feared that if he were to break into a run that something might run out of those houses and devour him alive.

Then the eyes were accompanied by soft whispers that disturbed the still and dusty air of the town. He felt that his presence there had somehow disturbed something dormant, and yet at the same time he felt as if he had been in a right place that commanded him to be there.

He walked onward and the eyes continued to observe and voices continued to whisper. Were they of people or of monsters? Get that stupid thought out of your head, Sam thought in in the confines of his head but knew that whatever was watching him from those homes and shops had heard him. Where was everyone? Was this just a dream, a very deep one for that matter, that he had trouble waking from? He continued to walk toward the church on the hill and at the same time hoped that each step would bring him closer to reality, to waking up in his bed, covered in cold sweat. But no such thing happened, so he was just left with his shaky legs to carry him to what he thought was his destination.

The clouds positioned themselves low above the city, so low that Sam thought he could even touch them if he extended his hand the full length. They looked like a dark, thick blanket that had covered this town in mystery. And yet the strangest thing about them was that they actually didn't move. They stood perfectly still in the same spot, stretching in all directions as far as the eye could see. He turned around completely, his gaze sweeping over the empty town in a circle, and realized that there was no breeze.

Everything was dormant.

After a few minutes, he had arrived in front of the church. The climb up the hill proved to be an exhausting task, breathing in the still and somewhat polluted air-it was the best way he could describe it-he felt as if he were missing a lung.

The church looked old, dirty, deteriorated. Its steeple was slanted, as if an earthquake had hit it some time ago and no one had ever bothered to fix it.

Sam planted his foot onto the first step of the wooden stairs that led to the front door under an equally slanted porch, and listened the old wood creak under his weight. He feared that is he took another step he would fall through. He jumped over the next three steps and found himself at the door. Was there any point in knocking, he thought as he raised his hand to just do such a thing. He thought better of it and reached for the rusty knob. It turned in his hand and the door creaked open, letting out a putrid stench.

Inside, the light was dim, just barely what came through the curtained, dusty windows. Though, there was just enough of it to show him the ghastly horror that stretched before him.

All down the hall hung clear body bags; each one of them was splattered in blood, gory contents clearly visible, the faces of victims forever frozen in horror, though each one of them was missing eyes. The bodies were decapitated in most gruesome ways imaginable, some missing arms, some legs, others all appendages and more.

Holding a hand over his mouth in an effort not to throw up, Sam went for the door but found it to be firmly shut. The knob wouldn't budge, as if it were forever shut. Come to think of it, he didn't even remember opening the door. Everything became a blur, a haze of terror and dread. He ran down the hall in the opposite direction, as fast as his weary legs could carry him. There was only one door on that shorter side of the hallway. He slammed into the door with his shoulder, and without any effort the door gave way under his force.

He slammed the door shut. It gave no echo, barely a dull sound that the church seemed to have absorbed in its fabric of existence. He went to the far wall, not that the room was large and sat in the corner. He realized the room was actually a bathroom; he sat in the corner where a tub could have been, pipes protruding from the blood-stained tiles. There was a toilet facing him from the other side and a half-broken sink.

Closing his eyes in an effort to escape this decrepit place, that was at one time or another supposed to be holy, he gave an exasperated sigh. Words escaped his closed lips. He prayed to find himself in his bed, prayed for the nightmare to be over. Yet when he opened his eyes, he found a man sitting on a toilet.

The man was naked, or so he thought, though there was no sure way of telling if this were true or not, for the man appeared to be burnt. His entire body was charred, as if someone had roasted him on an open fire, turned him on a spike over and over again until every inch of his body was shriveled in the flames. He sat in an upright position, almost at a ninety-degree angle, a position that made him look very attentive.

Sam froze in horror.

"You came to the right place," the man said and his head turned to Sam. "She's been waiting for you. You have to go and see her." The man chuckled, like a mad man, sounding almost like a hyena when it knows it's about to devour its prey.

"What?" Sam barely manage to form his thoughts into a single word.

"She's been waiting for you for so long. She told us so much about you, and, well, to tell you the truth, we've been all dying to meet you. Literally!" The man burst into laughter, a crazed, demented laughter that was too, absorbed by the building.

"Who's been waiting? What-"

"No time for that. Hurry on down the hall. Pass those poor, unfortunate ones that were judged first. Sad fate had befallen them, I'll tell you that much. Me? Well at least I get to sit here and chew the fat with the likes of you."

"I'm sorry-"

"Tell me something, Sam, do you like chewing the fat?" The man opened his mouth wide open, revealing his rotten, black teeth with pieces of meet hanging in between them. "I'll tell you, it's finger lickin' good!" He put his hand in his mouth and began to chew on it, biting off each finger and then the hand itself, until his entire arm was down his mouth being eaten.

Sam covered his eyes and began to scream and when he opened them, the man was gone. In the place where he sat was a piece of paper. Sam scurried over to it and took it into his shaky hands. It was a note, written in what clearly looked like Jackie's handwriting. It read:

Sam, I've been waiting for you. I can't stay here long. I'm really scared of this place. There is something so terrible here and I think it's looking for me and when it finds me, it will eat me. I know it will, Sam.
Please, if you're coming, hurry! I have to go now! I will wait for you in the main hall. It's past those awful body bags.

-Jackie

His hands trembled even harder as he finished reading the note. A tear ran down his cheek. He wiped it with the sleeve of his shirt and walked out of the nightmarish bathroom. Tucking the note in his back pocket, he walked down the hall, but slowed down considerably when he reached the body bags.

Reluctantly, tiny step followed by another tiny step, he waked by them. One of them wriggled suspended in the air and let out an agonizing, painful moan that stayed in the bloody plastic bag.

This prompted Sam to run faster, past the suspended bodies until they were far behind him.

Gasping for air, he reached the main hall, or at least what looked to be a main hall. The door leading into it was already torn down, cut down it's what it looked like. The pews were crookedly lined up, some half broken off, as if some crazed animal had chewed on it.

At the altar stood a woman.

Even through dim light and stark shadows created by the oversized, half melted, candles, Sam could see that the woman was in fact Jackie. She stood there, her arms at her sides, head pointed downward in a sad gaze. He ran to her, and when he got to her, he hugged her. He hugged her so hard that he lifted her off the ground and at the same time feared he would squeeze all the life out of her.

"Oh, I can't believe I have found you!" He exclaimed, joy and shock slowly mixing. "I've been looking for you for so long, I have, I have, I swear I have. I didn't know where else to look for."

Jackie slowly stretched her arms out to wrap them around Sam. "I've been waiting for you, Sam."

"I know, I know you have. And I'm sorry. Oh god, how I've missed you."

"Well, you've found me."

He stopped hugging her and pushed her away a little to take a good look at her. He wiped her dirty face and smiled. "I didn't even know this place existed. Where are we?"

She looked at him, all sickly and pale. Her long black hair that had incredible lust and shine to it was now just hanging off her head like strands of hay. She was thin. Bones protruded from every joint, every limb that Sam could touch and feel its coldness.

"What happened to you?" Sam said as he kiss her on the forehead.

Jackie smiled, though the smile was not warm. It wasn't pleasant. It revealed her dark, stained teeth and discolored tongue. "You really don't remember?" She said weakly.

"What are you talking about?" Sam asked confused.

She fell silent.

"What are you talking about?" He repeated.

"You really don't remember what happened? Doesn't this place look familiar to you?"

"This church? I don't know, I've never even seen this church. And it looks like everyone in town just got up and left."

"Look behind you, Sam?"

He turned and to his surprise, to his horror, he saw pews filled with people.

"Those are the people that came to our wedding, Sam. You still don't remember? This is the church we got married in."

Sam took a step back. All the strength he thought he had regained was once again drained from his body. He felt light headed, the whirlwind in his skill rendering him almost unconscious. He knew something, thought what that was remained an utter mystery to him. It gnawed at him, at his psyche; the town he thought to be empty, the charred man who ate himself, the people now who came to see them, who were actually at their wedding. Jackie stood there still and he could almost feel her tug at his sanity, tug at his nerves, forcing him to admit the truth.

"What happened, Jackie?" He said, tears running down his face, fearing he knew the answer.

"You killed me, my love. You killed me and hid my body in our back yard, right by the oak tree that casts that brilliant shadow over our house. You remember the oak tree? Do you remember how I used to be scared because I said it's branches at night look like evil hands out to get me? Do you remember that?"

Now he remembered killing her. It hit him hard, right in the face, like a gust of wind that took his breath away.

"You killed me and kicked me out of your memory, kicked the murder you committed out of your mind, and you've left me here in my own hell to rot. To eat myself away out of existence completely. But I can't let that happen until I erase you along with me."

Sam began to keel over but her frail hand held his chin up, somehow still keeping him standing.

"Embrace me now," she said as Sam began to sob.

"I'm sorry...I'm really sorry."

"Embrace me and let us burn. Let us burn together."

"I'm afraid," snot ran down his chin, his voice gurgling in his own saliva as he sobbed.

"I know you are. It will hurt. Feeling the flames on your body as it crawls over and you feel a million little stings that pick your skin away. It hurts, your flesh being melted away."

He slowly approached her and cowered into her open arms. She hugged him and he began to burn, and she with him.

His sobs turned into screams as she stepped away and watched her once husband be engulfed in flames, in thick, orange flames that at him away, ate him away out of existence. He cried in agony until his body became still and there was no voice coming from his cooked insides.

He woke up at the beginning of the street and looked at the church on the hill.

He saw the houses, now recognizing all of them.

The voice called. He couldn't resist.

Punishment awaited and he was its eternal prisoner.

The End.

Emir Skalonja

My name is Emir Skalonja. I was born in 1987, in Sarajevo, Bosnia and Herzegovina. In 2002, at the age of 14, I left Bosnia and Herzegovina and settled in Buffalo, New York, United States. I attended University at Buffalo where I studied History and Film. I graduated in 2010.

I married Nicole Buergin on September 21st, 2013, and so far…marriage rocks! My wife Nicole is my go to person for editing and proofreading. All story ideas are introduced to her first.

I am an emerging writer; my first short story, Darkness, was published by Death Throes Publishing in an anthology titled Peripheral Distortions, in January of 2014. My newest story, Fragments, appearing in Sanitarium is my second story to be published, and most certainly not the last.

My aspirations are to become a renowned writer, whether it be as a novelist or in film.

I recently submitted a short comic script to 2000 A.D. for their Future Shocks feature, and am currently in the process of finalizing my first novel titled Gabriel.

CLAYTON HILL SANITARIUM

Requiescat

Charles Martin

Dedicated to the memory of Edgar Allan Poe.

YOU MUST UNDERSTAND: IT WAS NOT INSANITY that drove me, but love. Insanity is contingent upon the sufferer's incapability of distinguishing between right and wrong. I know what I did was wrong, therefore I cannot be insane. It was wrong. Monstrous, you might say, but what does love care for right and wrong? Love is above such things. All is pure in the eyes of love. People who read this account and deem me insane know nothing of love, and they are wretched creatures for it.

Oh, how I have loved my Emalain. From the moment my parents brought her home, a poor, orphaned waif, and announced that she was to be my sister I loved her. We grew together, and with growth came the certainty that there was not anywhere in the world a match for my Emalain. People talk of beauty (poets and artists have striven to capture its essence), but they have not seen my Emalain resplendent with blossoming womanhood. People talk of strength, but they have never spoken with my Emalain; I cannot think of one person who long held their own in an argument with her.

We grew, and my love was stronger with each passing year.

I never once let her know, of course. I was quite careful about that. Never, by either word or gesture, did I betray what was in my heart. I have always had a great knack for self-containment and this virtue served me well when, in her sixteenth year (my twentieth), Emalain introduced me to her betrothed; a gentleman whose acquaintance she had made while on holiday.

The bitterness and anger I felt in those moments are not within my power to describe. The best I can do is to say they burned the back of my throat like bile; crippled my heart like a cancer.

But I hid it well, and assured them, as Emalain's brother and lord of the manor (our parents having passed several years before), that my blessing was theirs.

But even from that moment, I had determined to keep her with me here, where my love would shelter her all the rest of our lives.

A ball must be arranged, I announced, to celebrate the betrothal.

'Oh, Simon,' my beloved said to me. 'You need not go to such trouble. Can't we just enjoy a small dinner...'

'Nonsense,' I said. 'If my Emalain is happy, then all must share in her happiness.'

She continued to resist, but under the sustained urgings from Arthur and myself, she was forced to relented, on the condition that we leave all arrangements to her. So, the date was set (three months thence – more than enough time to set my plan in motion) and invitations raced through the upper echelons of society.

What a ball it was! The music, the food, the dancing... never before or since had I been a spectator to such gaiety. But I was a phantom amongst them; a cipher, watching as they gorged and besotted themselves, as the cultured are wont to do when there are no outsiders to pass judgement.

And then she came to me. Oh, you should have seen her, her white dress a magnificent precursor to her bridal gown, our mother's jewels shining like stars in the mantle of her hair. She came to me laughing and, taking my hands in hers, kissed my face, and blessed me for being so good to her and for my kindness to her fiancé. No one had ever had a better brother, she said.

I knew, then, that the time had come.

I bade her follow me into an adjoining dining chamber where I had ordered a servant place a decanter of wine and two glasses. Here we were perfectly alone.

I approached the table and poured the wine.

'To Emalain,' I raised my glass. 'May...'

'To Simon,' she interrupted my speech, clinking her glass against mine. 'May happiness follow him all the days of his life.'

We smiled and drank.

'We had better be getting back,' she set her glass down and turned to leave. 'Arthur will...'

She staggered, clutching hold of a chair in an effort to remain upright. The drug I had mixed with her wine was a fast worker. She slurred a few words more before her legs melted out from under her. I rushed forward to catch her and gathered her up in my arms.

The first stage of my plan was accomplished. Now for the rest.

Behind a high portrait in that room is the secret passage. Gaining this, I bore my beloved down to the network of cellars lying under the manor; the crumbling remnants of a castle that once stood on the sight of my family home. People seldom ventured into these vaults, and even then not too deeply. Such old places are treacherous, you see? Walls and ceilings conspire to fall without a moment's notice upon the unsuspecting venturer. But she would be safe down here.

I was certain of that.

Torches, lit and set by myself earlier that night, showed the way through those subterranean labyrinths.

At last we came to the place. In a dark, forgotten corner of the cellars, between two ancient walls, was a deep niche wherein I laid her down. Then I went to work fastening about her arms and waist the chains I had spent the last month setting into the masonry. She would be safe here. Nothing would touch her here. Nothing and no one.

Near at hand was the pile of bricks, mortar, and masonry tools which would ensure my beloved's eternal safety. I set myself to work, piling brick upon brick. It was hurried work, and sloppy, I admit, but the wall need not be strong, it need only remain upright.

The wall was level with my chest when I heard a sound that chilled my blood: the clank of chains and a groan from my beloved.

I froze, a brick in one hand, trowel in the other. The drug was wearing off!

'What...' she murmured, raising a manacled wrist to rub at her eyes. 'What's going on? Where... Simon?'

Quick! I must finish!

I resumed my work and it is only here that I will make an admission to a flash of madness, but it was more to do with the frantic manner in which I manipulated the bricks and mortar than my actual state of mind. I was not insane. I am not insane!

'Simon?' the chains rattled as she staggered to her feet. 'Simon, what is going on? What is all this? I... Oh my god. Simon, stop. Stop this, right now! This isn't funny!' Pulled taut, the chains would not permit her to move more than a pace or two forward. 'Simon! Simon, are you listening to me? Let me out of here! Simon? Simon, look at me!'

I worked faster.

Five bricks more. Just five bricks more.

'Simon,' she was panicking now. 'Oh my god, Simon, please.'

'Please, Emmy,' I said. 'Don't make this harder than it is. It's for your own good. You'll see.'

'Oh, Simon,' she sobbed, and the sound hit me like a blow to the heart. 'Simon, please. I don't understand. I'm very frightened right now. Please, just let me out and... and we can talk.' She reached her hands towards me as far the chains would allow. 'Please Simon.

Please, I want to go home. Oh, please...'

I never paused. She was home. Could she not see that? She would always be home now.

'ARTHUR!' she screamed for her fiancé, and my heart bled. 'ARTHUR! HELP! SOMEONE PLEASE HELP!'

'One day,' I think I whispered as the wall neared completion. 'One day, you'll understand.'

Her words degenerated into a frenzy of babbles, screams, and sobs as I pressed the last brick into place. And above it all was the jangling of chains, like the thrashing of a mad ghost from one of those dreadful horror novels she enjoyed so much.

My work done, I hastened from the cellars, extinguishing torches as I went. Her screams and pleas to be released from the dark and dust hounded me, but I quickly outpaced them, and the only sound to be heard when I regained the dining room was that of a party that had reached its crescendo.

I closed the portrait, secured it, and returned to our guests.

'Simon,' Arthur came up to me, laying his arm across my shoulders.

'I've been looking all over for you. Have you seen Emmy?' I told him I had not, but that she should be about.

'Sure, sure,' he smiled. 'But come, have a drink with me. I've been imposing on your hospitality for over three months and I don't think we've ever drank together.'

I accepted the invitation, feeling better disposed towards him now that I knew she would never be his. We talked for close to an hour of life, the past, and the great hopes he harboured for the future of our families.

'But, drat,' he said at one point. 'Where is Emmy?'

At length, it was discovered that Emalain was not to be found anywhere within the manor. It was suggested the we search the grounds, a task which consumed the better part of three hours, by which time Arthur had become quite distraught and I was forced to call an early end to the festivities.

I will not bother with the details of what came after. Any of the old folk in the village can tell you of the great search parties Arthur and myself sent far and wide over the moors and valleys, combing for the smallest clue that might shed light on what had become of Emalain. The King himself could not have mustered so grand a force.

Poor Arthur was a wreck. I let him abide in the manor while we searched, but after months without sight or word, he simply had to accept that Emalain was lost to him. He left me a wretched shell of the man that had first alighted on my doorstep, arm-in-arm with my beloved.

I did not despair at his leaving, and, in the forty years since, I have never wondered what became of him. There is talk of alcoholism and the ruination of his estate, but I care not.

Nor have I been down to those cellars. Heaven knows I have wanted to go. But there is a ghoulishness about that painting and its secret passage which arrests me whenever I draw near and I have to flee that room. I do not think it is fear, though I will admit to having not been comfortable in the dark for many years now, and the sound of chains grates terribly on my nerves.

I cannot say what it is, but my account is finished and I will recall no more.

So, you see? I am not insane. What I did, I did out of love. Was it selfish? I suppose. But is that not the greatest of loves: the love that will have all or nothing? Who can say that they have loved as I have loved? Who among you would make themselves into monsters in the name of their love? You, with your tinsel affections! Your loves are sand and dust. Mine is deep as the bones of the earth and eternal as the darkness beyond death.

Oh, my Emalain...

The End.

Case #64570

Charles Martin

Charles Martin is a procrastinator par excellence who has never quite managed to get the hang of adulthood. He is a lover of films (particularly the animated sort), reading, video games, and heavy metal music.

When it comes to horror fiction, he admires the works of Edgar Allan Poe, Shirley Jackson, Stephen King, and H. P. Lovecraft. Films like Nosferatu, The Exorcist, and The Shining, are also a big influence.

His hobbies include film reviewing and blasting heavy metal at the highest possible volume.

Dark Verse

Physician: Dr. Salam
7128-DV758JJ

Lex Sinclair
Cindy Morren
M. Brett Gaffney

Day by day I gazed upon it,
through my bedroom window,
in the windswept pasture below.
There stood, arms spread out, the scarecrow;
rocking gently to and fro in the chilly gale,
whipping from the shore.
He stood towering over the overgrown corn, Evermore.

The Scarecrow sustained all weathers.
Never once moving, nor speaking,
but I could hear him whispering something
unintelligible all the more.
Beneath the brim of his fedora, the toothless mouth
grinned at me; its protruding eyes milky white,
shining in the gloom of night.

Day by day I gazed upon the Scarecrow,
hoping, pleading that it was there no more.
But it stood unmoving,
its eyes meeting mine through the rattling pane,
assailed by the winter storm.

That night as I lay not sleeping,
but tired, bone-weary more and more,
I heard loud scraping on my window.
Too frightened was I to sit upright and see was the cause.

Then by the dim, grey light of dawn,
welcomed by the dulcet singing of the sparrows,
I woke; though I recall nothing of my dreamless slumber,
save the scraping, echoing in my mind.

When I gazed out the window,
to the pasture below, I saw no Scarecrow waiting,
neither fallen on the earth's meadow floor.
The Scarecrow stood, unmoving in the field Nevermore,
for it stood right behind me, grinning its toothless grin,
evermore.

Case #65054

Lex Sinclair

Lex Sinclair was born in Wales, United Kingdom in 1983. He is the author of five horror/suspense novels such as, Nobody Goes There, The Lord of Darkness, Killer Spiders, The Goat's Head & the sequel Neighbourhood Watch. Some of his short stories have appeared in previous Sanitarium magazine issues, where he hopes to publish more. In 2010 his short story The Dies is Cast received Runners-Up Prize in the Terry Hetherington Young Writers Award. His poetry has appeared in anthologies and The South Wales Evening Post.

Also, his novels The One Eyed Monster, Abducted & I Wish have been earmarked for publication in the foreseeable future, along with the trilogy series Don't Fear The Reaper.

He currently resides in Skewen, Wales where he is busy working on his next writing project. He is proud to be part of Sanitarium issue 21.

All his novels are available on Amazon and other web sites.

How lonely is the cripple
Up there in his chair
Peering into the night
Through the window upstairs

A shadow in the dark
Watching others in the park
From his chair he would stare
At the girl with long brown hair

And she had seen him too
Through the mornings' dew
But neither she nor anyone else knew
That he was no more than twenty -two

A young killer was he
So one night, regretfully
She had stopped to see
What appeared to be, a cripple crying out
"Please help me"

And kindly she did
But through her side- the knife slid
Tears welled in her eyes
As he laughed through the disguise

On his shoes -her blood stippled
In his ear - her scream rippled
A song of death played on the
fiddle How beguiling is the cripple

Case #35211

Cindy Morren

Cindy Morren lives in New York where she studies English and minors in Psychology. When she is not being studious, she enjoys writing anything that comes to her dark and exquisitely sinister mind.

CLAYTON HILL SANITARIUM

You never think it's going to be you. School shootings, bank robberies, zombies, whatever. Those things happen to other people. And yet, here I am, cameraman on the scene of what looks to be a total clusterfuck.

When I was a kid, I took some photos of this car accident in front of my house. While my Mom called an ambulance, I circled the truck, its entrails spun out on the asphalt like dirty ribbon. The people inside were quiet, their faces hidden in the airbags. I don't remember how many pictures I caught, but I never let go of the camera. Without all the sirens and stretchers and medics it was like it wasn't real, but maybe a dream or a movie I'd watched one night after my parents went to bed, a movie I wasn't supposed to see. I don't know but maybe that's why I got the gig with this news channel, so I can view the world and all its mess through a lens, as if that can keep the monsters away, as if when the terror turns its sights on me, I can stop recording and go home.

A woman shouts, tells me to tape everything for fuck's sake, tape it all so that someone can see what's happened here, and so I do: blood like paint around the mouth, screams come in from outside the frame like they're an audience, timed applause, and when we run, we run on cue,

we fall down, get shot, bleed out, and die like stars, each of us our own bright moment on the screen, everyone an ending but me. But it's okay, it's okay because it's a movie and when the credits roll, they'll find my name.

Case #38792

M. Brett Gaffney

M. Brett Gaffney, born in Houston, Texas, holds an MFA in poetry from Southern Illinois University and is an associate editor for Gingerbread House literary magazine. Her poems have appeared or are forthcoming in The Medulla Review, Newfound, Ruminate, Psaltery & Lyre, Stone Highway Review, Slipstream, Wind, Penduline, Cactus Heart, Exit 7, REAL, Still, Licking River Review, and Permafrost. Her favorite things include horror movies, ping-pong, stingrays, and Halloween, a holiday she plans for year-round.

Gingerbread House literary magazine: http://gingerbreadhouselitmag.com/

CLAYTON HILL SANITARIUM

On the
Record

THIS ISSUE WE HAD A CHANCE TO SIT down with one third of the self-publishing podcast team Sean Platt.

The guys are putting the finishing touches to their already funded Kickstarter project "Fiction unboxed". 30 days, 75,000 words - all live!

So sit back and enjoy the ride.

How do you feel the industry has changed since your first release?

All in all I think the industry is stronger, smarter and more capable than it was when we first published Yesterday's Gone Season One. While I still think it's mostly frontier, many authors now publishing to Kindle and other e-reader platforms are more educated, driven and focused. The industry is more competitive in the best possible way. I would imagine that most of the "Kindle Gold Rush" type of writer

— those just in it for the easy dollar — are already gone, leaving the field to serious authors who want to create superior work.

Beyond that, algorithms have evolved, and it is probably more difficult for the average author to get noticed, but I also believe that the higher quality the average e-book, the more likely readers will be to develop a regular habit.

With all that is going on around you, how do you stay focused on one project?

I've never stayed focused on a single project in my life, and long ago stopped trying. I do my best to look at the big picture, from that day's work to the next quarter's waiting queue, and determine my most important tasks (immediate requirements) needed to move me from A to Z.

I have no ability to focus on a single project, but am trained on one project per vertical — that means one project with Dave, one project with Johnny, and usually one other thing (like something for Guy Incognito).

Do you personally have a favourite genre to write in?

Not at all. It's easy for me to get excited by whatever I'm working on at any given time. As a general rule I enjoy fiction more than nonfiction, but personal responses to nonfiction can be more rewarding.

Out of the worlds that you have created (of which there are many), who is your favourite character?

Boricio from Yesterday's Gone, by far. I love many of our characters, but Boricio has a voice that is tremendous fun to write in. And it comes in small doses, so I never tire of it. You hear actors say that playing the bad guy is always more fun. I feel the same way about writing them.

With that in mind, if you have the chance, would you re-write any of your current characters?

No, and it isn't because I think we have perfect characters. I just don't like changing history. Having said that, there is something I wish I'd written better. In Yesterday's Gone's first season Luca is written slightly infantile. This was by design, Luca was based on my son, Ethan, and he regresses when scared. It's how he deals with things. I wouldn't change that in the story, but I would do a better job of making it clear to the reader.

Of your releases, which is the stand out cover for you?

Unicorn Western, without a doubt. I love that cover with all my heart. I think the original Yesterday's Gone cover is epic, especially considering it was the second thing Dave and I did. But Unicorn Western is magical. That book takes a stupid idea and makes it epic, the cover conveys that immediately.

Fiction format seems to be in a constant state of flux (episodes, series, novellas, shorts and of course novels). Which do you prefer writing?

I don't have a preference. It's important that we always run with the most appropriate format for a particular narrative, but I don't necessarily like writing one more than the other. I enjoy the serial format because you can open so many boxes and are under no obligation to close them all, at least not until you finish the series. This flexibility opens doors for some truly creative storytelling, and that is often thrilling. I also like short stories. I wish I wrote more novels, but I'm doing something about it. Both the Inkwell and R&S have stand-alone novels coming out, and the three of us are excited to write more.

After the drafts, editing and final polish, once you hit publish – have you ever had a WTF moment with a glaring error? If so, how did you deal with it?

Yes, a couple of times. With our speed and lack of beta readers, this is natural. It becomes part of the art. We turn mistakes into components of our story. Turning things around like that is a lot of fun.

Two years, dozens of books and series what keeps you going?

I really love what I do. I always have stuff always falling off my plate, but even tired I wake up excited. I get to tell stories for a living, and have no complaints. I love every part of the process, so excitement is easy. And it seems like the more I do, the more I want to do, I imagine momentum will be simple enough to maintain so long as I continue to only work on projects that I love.

If something was to happen to any of you, what happens to the IP's and work you have created?

We all trust that each of us would do the honorable, responsible thing no matter what happens.

How difficult / easy was it to start working together and were there any fights for creative control?

Working together is ridiculously easy. Both are equally Awesome. I'm lucky to have such compatible partners. The guys are my brothers and we've not had A single fight for creative control among us.

With that in mind, have there been any "I told you so" moments?

Only in jest. Everyone likes being right, but we never rub it in one another's faces.

With regards to Fiction Unboxed, on scale of 1-10 how shit scared are you on starting this project?

I'd say a 6, and Johnny less than me. I think I'll find my feet almost immediately, and everything will be fine. But the anxiety leading up to it, well, I wish it was June 1 already. I normally write beats well ahead of a project. And before I write the beats, I have time to think about the story, characters, and setting. This time I have none of that. I'll have to poop beats and get Johnny started. It's part of the art this time, and I am comfortable with that, but will be slightly nervous until the story is actually started.

You have mentioned that a few sections will be crowd sourced voting (genre, setting etc.) Will there be any vetoing from you guys (I.e. Boricio Wolf goes to Disney for a "fun" time)

Yes, because I think it would be a bad idea to take every idea wholesale. Ultimately, people signed up to watch us right the best story we could in the least amount of time possible. That's exciting, and I don't think it would serve anyone to dilute that experience. It's most important to maintain the integrity of the story, so while we are interested and eager to absorb participant feedback, something that threatened the story's integrity would have to be vetoed.

Finally 30 days and 75,000+ words, which is more daunting?

Definitely 30 days. 75,000 words is a lot, sure, but we've done that before. Given it's ideal timeline this project would last 90 days. We're compressing quite a lot. But again, this time that's part of the art. Fortunately, we've been doing this for a year now and I trust our process. The 75,000 words will be relatively simple once we're going, but the 30 days will make it feel like a constantly ticking clock.
Hopefully, that will make it exciting for people to watch.

About Sean:

Sean loves writing books, even more than reading them. He is co-founder of Collective Inkwell and Realm & Sands imprints, writes for children under the name Guy Incognito, and has more than his share of nose.

Together with co-authors David Wright and Johnny B. Truant, Sean has written the series Yesterdays Gone, WhiteSpace, ForNevermore, Available Darkness, Dark Crossings, Unicorn Western, The Beam, Namaste, Robot Proletariat, Cursed, Greens, Space Shuttle, and Everyone Gets Divorced. He also co-wrote the how-to indie book, Write. Publish. Repeat.

http://collectiveinkwell.com

Can you describe what your workspace is like?

My workspace is very casual – it's just a corner of my bedroom where I have my laptops set up, and a cushion to sit on. I can just pop in my headphones and write away without anyone bothering me.

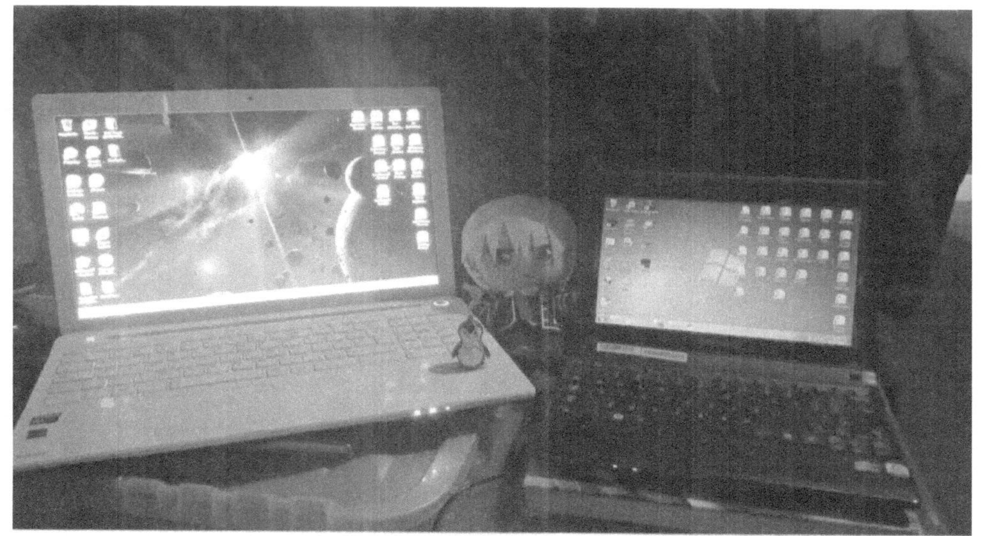

Do you have a go-to gadget / app or service that you cannot live without?

Besides the magical place called Spar, where I get my constant Coca-cola supply? Not really. All I need when I write is some rock music and caffeine.

Do you have a set routine while you work?

Nope. I just sit down and go. Sometimes I'll sit down to write, and when I look up, it's been six hours and my stomach is rumbling at me. Although, if anyone disturbs me while I'm working, I'm likely to bite their head off. Inspiration is very fickle and the two seconds it takes to tell someone to go away can be the two seconds it takes to lose my train of thought.

What is the best piece of advice you have ever received?

The best advice I ever got was actually from my best friend, and it was simply this: keep writing. Any time I feel like giving up, she encourages me to keep going – not for my readers, but for myself. I love writing, and though it can be stressful, I wouldn't want to do anything else.

Do you have a final piece of advice for our readers?

Keep trying. It doesn't matter what you're doing; if you're a writer, an artist, or just someone trying to get along in life, don't let a bump in the road, or someone's criticism, keep you down. Say a publisher turns you down, or you don't get the job you were going for – it's not the end of the world. It just means it wasn't the right fit for you. Keep looking, and you'll find where you're supposed to be.

About:

H.G. Lynch is an introverted Scottish pixie with too many voices in her head and a disturbing sense of humour. She enjoys

walks in the rain and watching horror movies. She had her first book, a vampire romance novel called Born Dark, published at eighteen, and her first horror novel, Insane, published at twenty. She can be found through Facebook, Twitter, or her website – www.hglynch. weebly.com

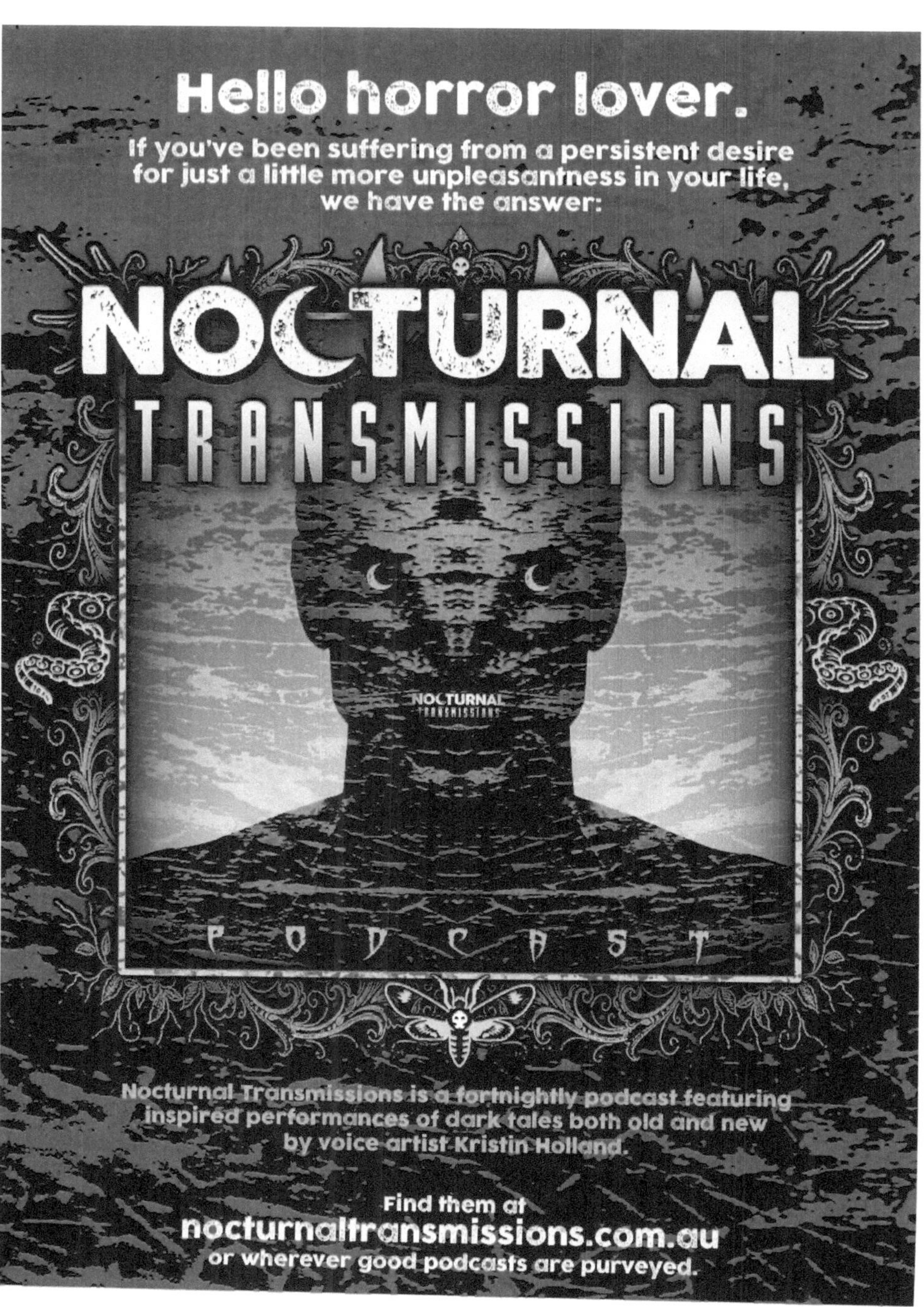

Hello horror lover.
If you've been suffering from a persistent desire
for just a little more unpleasantness in your life,
we have the answer:

NOCTURNAL
TRANSMISSIONS

NOCTURNAL
TRANSMISSIONS

PODCAST

Nocturnal Transmissions is a fortnightly podcast featuring
inspired performances of dark tales both old and new
by voice artist Kristin Holland.

Find them at
nocturnaltransmissions.com.au
or wherever good podcasts are purveyed.

If you have any feedback or would like to leave a review please head over to Amazon and share your thoughts about Sanitarium.

Thank you for your time and we salute your love for all things horror.

www.ingramcontent.com/pod-product-compliance
Lightning Source LLC
Chambersburg PA
CBHW020718160726

47993CB00006B/2255